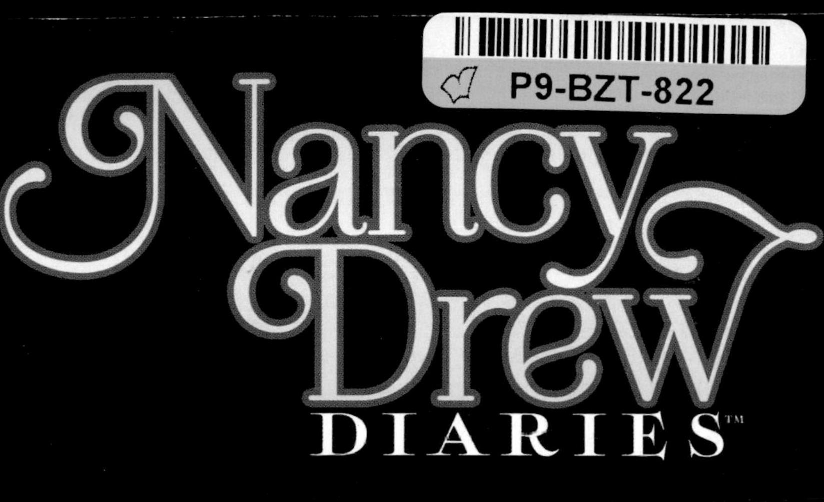

Nancy Drew DIARIES™

"A blood-curdling scream from down the hall made me wonder if anyone was taking the good news well."

–Nancy Drew

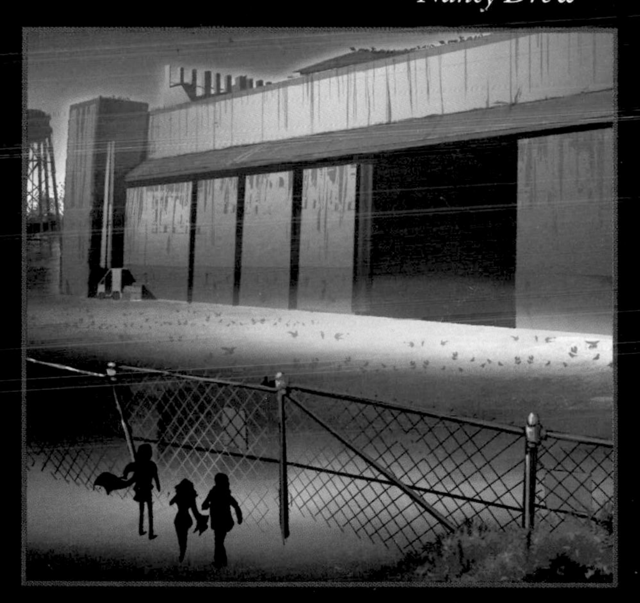

PAPERCUTZ

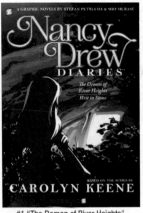

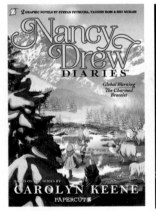

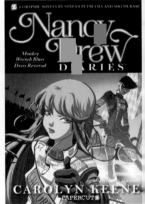

#5 "Ghost in the Machinery"
and
"Disoriented Express"

Based on the series by
CAROLYN KEENE

STEFAN PETRUCHA & SARAH KINNEY • Writers
SHO MURASE • Artist
with 3D CG elements and color by CARLOS JOSE GUZMAN

PAPERCUTZ™
New York

Nancy Drew Diaries
#5

"Ghost in the Machinery" and "Disoriented Express"
STEFAN PETRUCHA & SARAH KINNEY – Writers
SHO MURASE – Artist
with 3D CG elements and color by CARLOS JOSE GUZMAN
BRYAN SENKA – Letterer
JEFF WHITMAN – Production Coordinator
SUZANNAH ROWNTREE – Associate Editor
JIM SALICRUP
Editor-in-Chief

ISBN: 978-1-62991-193-9

Published by arrangement with Aladdin Paperbacks,
an imprint of Simon & Schuster Children's Publishing Division.

Printed in China

Distributed by Macmillian
First Printing

NANCY DREW HERE, IN THE WOODS, ENJOYING NATURE, AND GRATEFUL TO WHATEVER CAVE PERSON HAD THE SENSE TO DISCOVER THAT WONDERFUL SOURCE OF HEAT WE NOW CALL FIRE!
UNFORTUNATELY, THIS CAMPFIRE DOESN'T HAVE LONG TO LIVE. I PLAN TO *MURDER* IT SHORTLY.
BRRR. NANCY, COULDN'T YOU HAVE PICKED A WARMER NIGHT TO ABSOLUTELY *INSIST* THAT WE GO CAMPING?
NANCY ISN'T HERE *JUST* FOR THE FRESH AIR. THERE ARE MUCH BETTER CAMPING SPOTS IN RIVER HEIGHTS, SO MY GUESS IS THERE'S SOME MYSTERY AFOOT.
I GUESS IT'S DARK ENOUGH NOW FOR MY *CONFESSION*. I READ IN THE PAPER THAT THE LOCALS HAVE BEEN REPORTING *STRANGE LIGHTS* IN THESE WOODS.
CHAPTER ONE:
I SEE THE LIGHT, BUT DOES IT SEE ME?

OKAY. I GET THAT YOU COULDN'T RESIST A MYSTERY. I DON'T GET WHY YOU'RE PUTTING OUT OUR FIRE.
SIMPLE! WE WON'T BE ABLE TO SEE THE MYSTERY LIGHTS UNLESS IT'S COMPLETELY DARK.
CLICK
SIGH
I SUPPOSE YOU WANT ME TO TURN THIS OFF TOO, SO WE CAN FIND THIS GHOST, PSYCHO-KILLER, OR MOST LIKELY, THE GHOST OF A PSYCHO KILLER?
YES. NOW, PLEASE. LUCKY THERE'S NO MOON TONIGHT.

WHAT ARE YOU WAITING FOR?
NOTHING! MY FLASHLIGHT IS OFF!
IT'S NOT ME!
OR ME!
THEN WHO... ?
PSYCHO-KILLER'S GHOST!
TIME TO GO.

YEAH, LET'S MOVE IT! QUICK!
YOU GOT IT! FOR A SECOND THERE, I WAS WORRIED YOU WERE GOING TO TRY TO HEAD *TOWARD* THE CREEPY THING!

NANCY?

OH, SHE *DID* MEAN WE SHOULD RUN *TOWARD* IT!
ARE YOU SURPRISED? THAT'S OUR GIRL!

WHAT DO YOU THINK IT IS?
HEY, IF WE KNEW, WE PROBABLY *WOULDN'T* BE FOLLOWING IT!
WELL, THE GOOD NEWS IS I *DON'T* THINK IT'S A UFO.
BUT, THAT STILL LEAVES *KILLER PSYCHO-GHOST* AS A LIKELY POSSIBILITY.
LOOK.
Keep Out!
WHAT IS *THAT*?!

THE OLD GOVERNMENT MUNITIONS FACTORY.
DURING WORLD WAR II, MILITARY FACTORIES AND TEST SITES WERE ESTABLISHED IN REMOTE SPOTS ALL OVER THE COUNTRY!
PRETTY CREEPY.
THE LIGHT'S HEADING INTO THAT ENTRANCE.

MOST WERE CLOSED AND FORGOTTEN DECADES AGO. THIS ONE WAS FORGOTTEN. SEEMS THERE WAS JUST TOO MUCH *PAPERWORK* AFTER THE SECOND WORLD WAR AND FOLKS WERE TOO BUSY CELEBRATING TO DO IT *ALL*.
WHEN SOMEONE BOUGHT THE PROPERTY THIS YEAR, THEY DECIDED TO LET THE NEW OWNERS PAY FOR DEMOLISHING IT. IT WAS SCHEDULED TO BE DESTROYED WITH EXPLOSIVES THE VERY NEXT DAY.

C'MON!
OH, NO! YOU'RE NOT THINKING OF GOING *IN THERE*?
THEY'RE BLOWING THIS PLACE UP TOMORROW!
THERE COULD BE *EXPLOSIVES* ALL OVER IT, SET WITH HAIR TRIGGERS!
BUT, BESS, WHAT IF THE *GHOST* IS MALE, FASCINATING AND SINGLE?
RIGHT, LIKE I'M GOING TO DATE A PSYCHO-KILLER GHOST!
SPEAKING OF WHICH, THAT'S *ANOTHER* REALLY GOOD REASON *NOT* TO GO OVER THAT FENCE!
HEY, WAIT FOR ME!

CAN WE TURN ON OUR FLASHLIGHTS NOW? I'D HATE TO TRIP OVER A *DETONATOR!*
NO. WE DON'T WANT TO BE *SEEN.*
THE LIGHT. IT'S GONE.
IS THAT GOOD OR BAD?
SHHH.

MY PALS, BESS AND GEORGE, DO ***LOTS*** OF THINGS ABOVE AND BEYOND THE CALL OF DUTY...

...AND I ***OFTEN*** LEAD THEM INTO DANGER BY MY OBSESSION WITH MYSTERY-SOLVING...

...SOMETIMES THE ***REAL MYSTERY*** IS WHY THEY HANG OUT WITH ME...
CREEAAK

AEEIII!
CRRAAAKKKK
ESPECIALLY WHEN I GET SO WRAPPED UP IN SEARCHING FOR CLUES, THAT I FORGET WHERE I AM.
LIKE IN AN OLD, ROTTING BUILDING!
NANCY, GET A GRIP!
WE GOT YOU!
UH-OH...
SO, I'M AWFULLY GLAD THEY DO STICK WITH ME.

BUT I'M NOT SURE IT'S THE *SMARTEST* THING THEY COULD DO.
EEEEAAAIIII!
WUMPH!
OOF!
THUD THUD THUD
MAYBE FOLLOWING SOMEONE INTO DEATH-DEFYING ADVENTURES AGAIN AND AGAIN IS WHAT FRIENDSHIP IS ALL ABOUT!
UNNNK.
IN FACT, I WAS THINKING HOW *SWELL* THEY WERE, JUST BEFORE I PASSED OUT! I DON'T KNOW *WHAT* THEY WERE THINKING OF ME.

WHEN I OPENED MY EYES, I WASN'T SURE WHERE I WAS.
THERE WAS A LIGHT. ANOTHER LIGHT.
THE PAIN IN MY BACK MADE ME DOUBT IT WAS A LIGHT FROM BEYOND, BECKONING ME TOWARD THE AFTERLIFE.
BUT THE GHOSTLY HAND THAT REACHED FOR ME MADE ME WONDER IF SOMEONE FROM THE AFTERLIFE WAS PAYING ME A VISIT.

UNFORTUNATELY, THERE WAS ONLY ONE WAY TO FIND OUT.
AND I CAN'T STAND LEAVING A MYSTERY UNSOLVED!
IF HE WAS A GHOST, HE SEEMED FRIENDLY ENOUGH—LIKE CASPER, ONLY HEAVIER.
HELLO THERE!
GOOD THING I WAS HERE. YOU GIRLS WERE IN A BIT OF A PICKLE!
ALWAYS A MISTAKE TO VENTURE DOWN A RABBIT HOLE IF YOU CAN'T GET OUT YOURSELF! HA-HA!

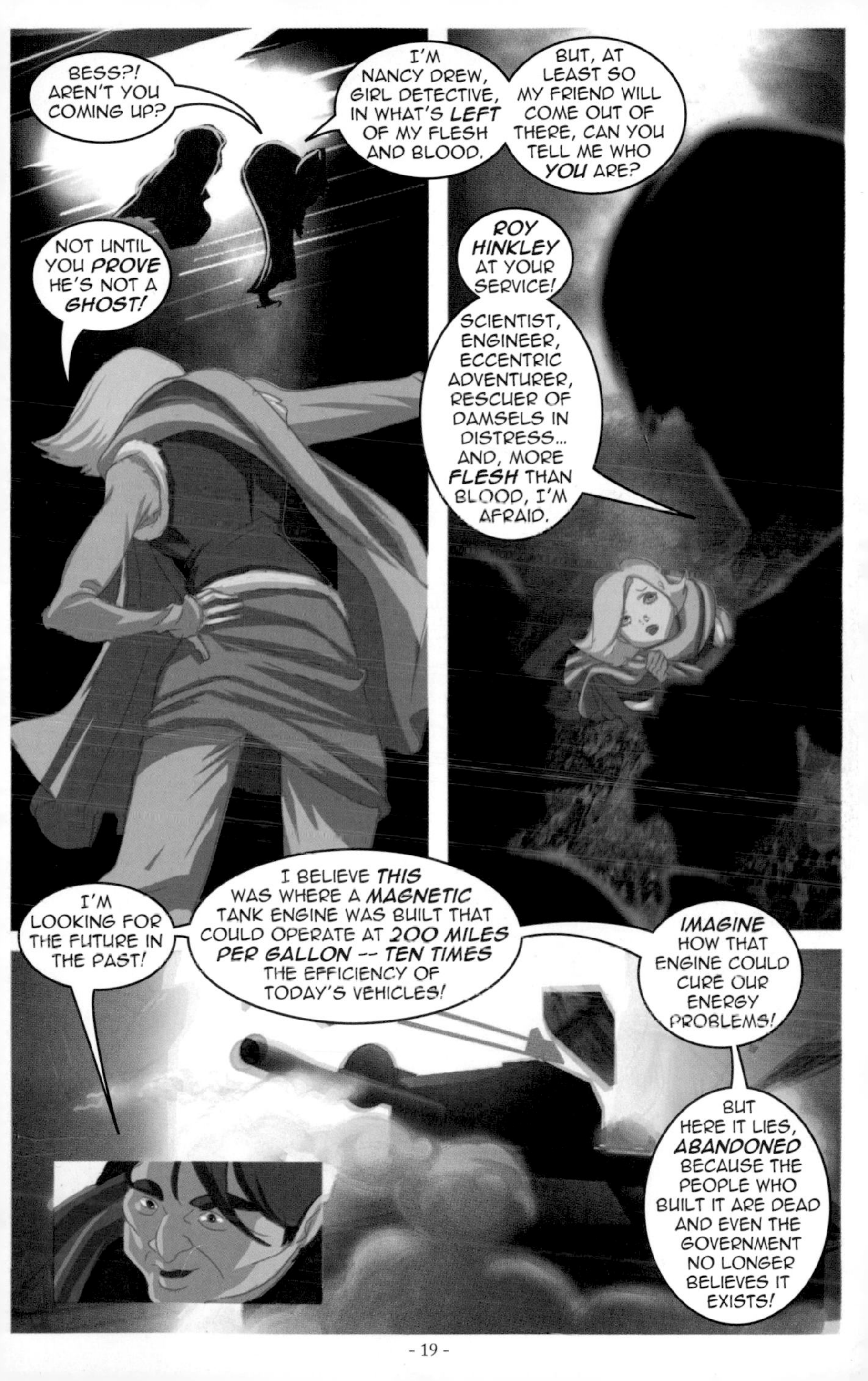
BESS?! AREN'T YOU COMING UP?
I'M NANCY DREW, GIRL DETECTIVE, IN WHAT'S LEFT OF MY FLESH AND BLOOD.
BUT, AT LEAST SO MY FRIEND WILL COME OUT OF THERE, CAN YOU TELL ME WHO YOU ARE?
NOT UNTIL YOU PROVE HE'S NOT A GHOST!
ROY HINKLEY AT YOUR SERVICE!
SCIENTIST, ENGINEER, ECCENTRIC ADVENTURER, RESCUER OF DAMSELS IN DISTRESS... AND, MORE FLESH THAN BLOOD, I'M AFRAID.
I'M LOOKING FOR THE FUTURE IN THE PAST!
I BELIEVE THIS WAS WHERE A MAGNETIC TANK ENGINE WAS BUILT THAT COULD OPERATE AT 200 MILES PER GALLON -- TEN TIMES THE EFFICIENCY OF TODAY'S VEHICLES!
IMAGINE HOW THAT ENGINE COULD CURE OUR ENERGY PROBLEMS!
BUT HERE IT LIES, ABANDONED BECAUSE THE PEOPLE WHO BUILT IT ARE DEAD AND EVEN THE GOVERNMENT NO LONGER BELIEVES IT EXISTS!

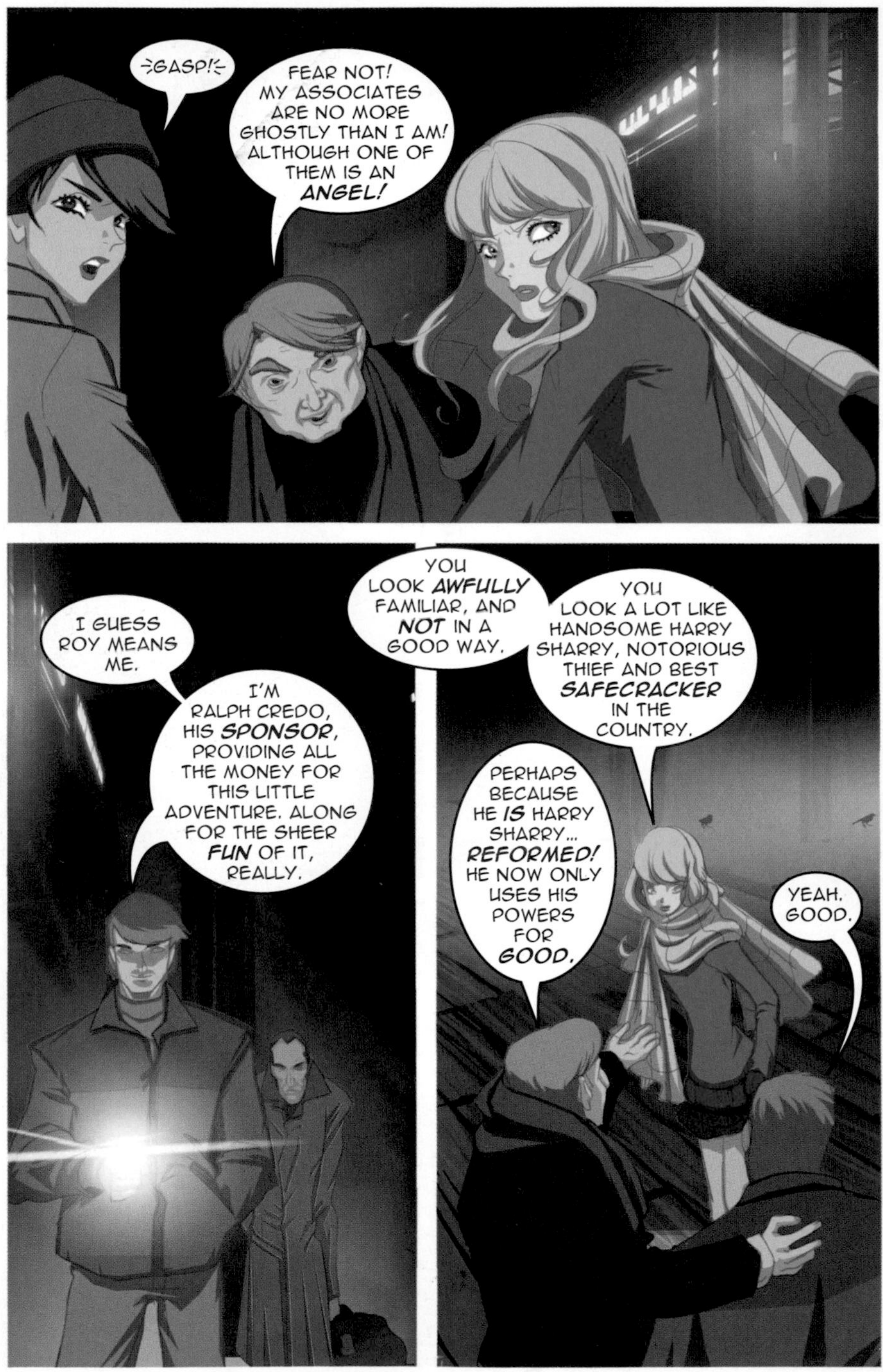
GASP!
FEAR NOT! MY ASSOCIATES ARE NO MORE GHOSTLY THAN I AM! ALTHOUGH ONE OF THEM IS AN ANGEL!
I GUESS ROY MEANS ME.
I'M RALPH CREDO, HIS SPONSOR, PROVIDING ALL THE MONEY FOR THIS LITTLE ADVENTURE. ALONG FOR THE SHEER FUN OF IT, REALLY.
YOU LOOK AWFULLY FAMILIAR, AND NOT IN A GOOD WAY.
YOU LOOK A LOT LIKE HANDSOME HARRY SHARRY, NOTORIOUS THIEF AND BEST SAFECRACKER IN THE COUNTRY.
PERHAPS BECAUSE HE IS HARRY SHARRY... REFORMED! HE NOW ONLY USES HIS POWERS FOR GOOD.
YEAH. GOOD.

BUT, HOW DO YOU KNOW THIS TANK EVER EXISTED, AND IF IT'S STILL *HERE*?
WELL, *SOMETHING'S* THROWING MY COMPASS INTO A SPIN. I'M HOPING IT'S THE ENGINE'S POWERFUL *MAGNETS*.
I TOLD THE GOVERNMENT ALL ABOUT IT, BUT RATHER THAN ADMIT MY CRAZY THEORY MIGHT BE RIGHT, THEY SOLD THE PLACE TO A DEVELOPER!
HE SAID WE CAN HELP OURSELVES TO ANY "URBAN LEGENDS" WE FIND. BEFORE HE BLOWS IT ALL UP... *TOMORROW*.
OKAY, SO MAYBE YOU'RE *NOT* GHOSTS.
CALL US WHATEVER YOU LIKE, DEAR GIRL. JUST NOT LATE FOR DINNER.
NOW, I HAVE TO WONDER WHAT NICE GIRLS LIKE *YOU* ARE DOING IN A PLACE LIKE THIS.

WE WERE INVESTIGATING A MYSTERIOUS LIGHT. BUT, *I'M* PRETTY SURE IT *WASN'T YOU*!
YOUR LIGHTS ARE WHITE. THE ONE WE FOLLOWED IN HERE WAS *GREEN*.
KIND OF LIKE *THAT* ONE!

WOW! CURIOSITY CERTAINLY GETS THE BEST OF HER, EH?
YEAH. NANCY RUSHES IN WHERE ANGELS... AND WELL, MOST ANYONE, FEAR TO TREAD.
WELL, THAT'S NOT GOOD!
BUMP
BUMP
BUMP
BUMP
BUMP
BUMP

OH!
UH, THANKS, ROY.
A PLEASURE. WHAT DO YOU SAY WE LEAVE THE NAUGHTY GHOST ALONE FOR NOW AND GO FIND THE TANK DIVISION BEFORE ANYTHING ELSE HAPPENS?
WELL, ROY'S TANK MYSTERY WAS AT LEAST AS INTERESTING AS MY GHOST, AND IT PROBABLY WOULDN'T THROW ANY TIRES AT ME, SO...?

THE PLACE TURNED OUT TO BE EVEN BIGGER THAN IT LOOKED. WE SEARCHED FOR ***HOURS*** THROUGH ROOM AFTER ROOM FILLED WITH OLD PIECES OF WAR TOYS.

ONE WAS LITTERED WITH PIECES OF PLANES LIKE THE ***MUSTANG,*** THE FASTEST FIGHTER IN THE SKY AND A VITAL TOOL FOR THE ALLIES BEATING THE NAZIS.

ROY WAS PRETTY SMART, BUT SOON HE LOOKED PRETTY LOST.

THE COMPASS IS SPINNING FASTER THAN A DERVISH AFTER A TURKISH ESPRESSO. WE ***MUST*** BE CLOSE TO THE TANK UNIT. HA!

AT LEAST ROY WAS ***CHEERY*** ABOUT THE WHOLE THING.

SKURNK
WHAT WAS *THAT*?!
PROBABLY A RAT. I HATE RATS! CAN'T WE JUST COME BACK DURING DAYLIGHT?
WE *COULD*, DEAR FELLOW, BUT THERE WILL ONLY BE DUST LEFT AFTER THE DEMOLITION!
P 02
HMMM. *THIS* IS INTERESTING. THE FLOOR IS DIFFERENT. NO MORE HARD-WOOD.
YES. THAT'S REINFORCED CONCRETE. STRONG ENOUGH TO HOLD UP... PERHAPS A TANK?!
SO LET'S FOLLOW IT...
RIGHT THERE WITH YOU, GIRL DETECTIVE! SOMETHING TELLS ME THIS LEADS RIGHT TO THE--

TANKS!
UH, SOMEONE'S NOT NEARLY SO HAPPY ABOUT OUR DISCOVERY! LOOK!
TALK ABOUT THE WRITING ON THE WALL...!

AS MUCH AS I'D LOVE TO GET A GOOD LOOK AT SOME OF THE INTERESTING MACHINERY IN HERE, MAYBE WE SHOULD GET OUT, LIKE IT SAYS.

OH, THAT'S PROBABLY JUST KIDS BEING CUTE. BESIDES, WE HAVEN'T FOUND THE MAGNETIC ENGINE, YET.

NONE OF THESE SEEM TO BE IT, ROY. MAYBE WE'RE NOT IN THE RIGHT ROOM.

THEY WOULDN'T KEEP SOMETHING THAT IMPORTANT OUT IN THE OPEN HERE, BUT THEY MIGHT KEEP IT...

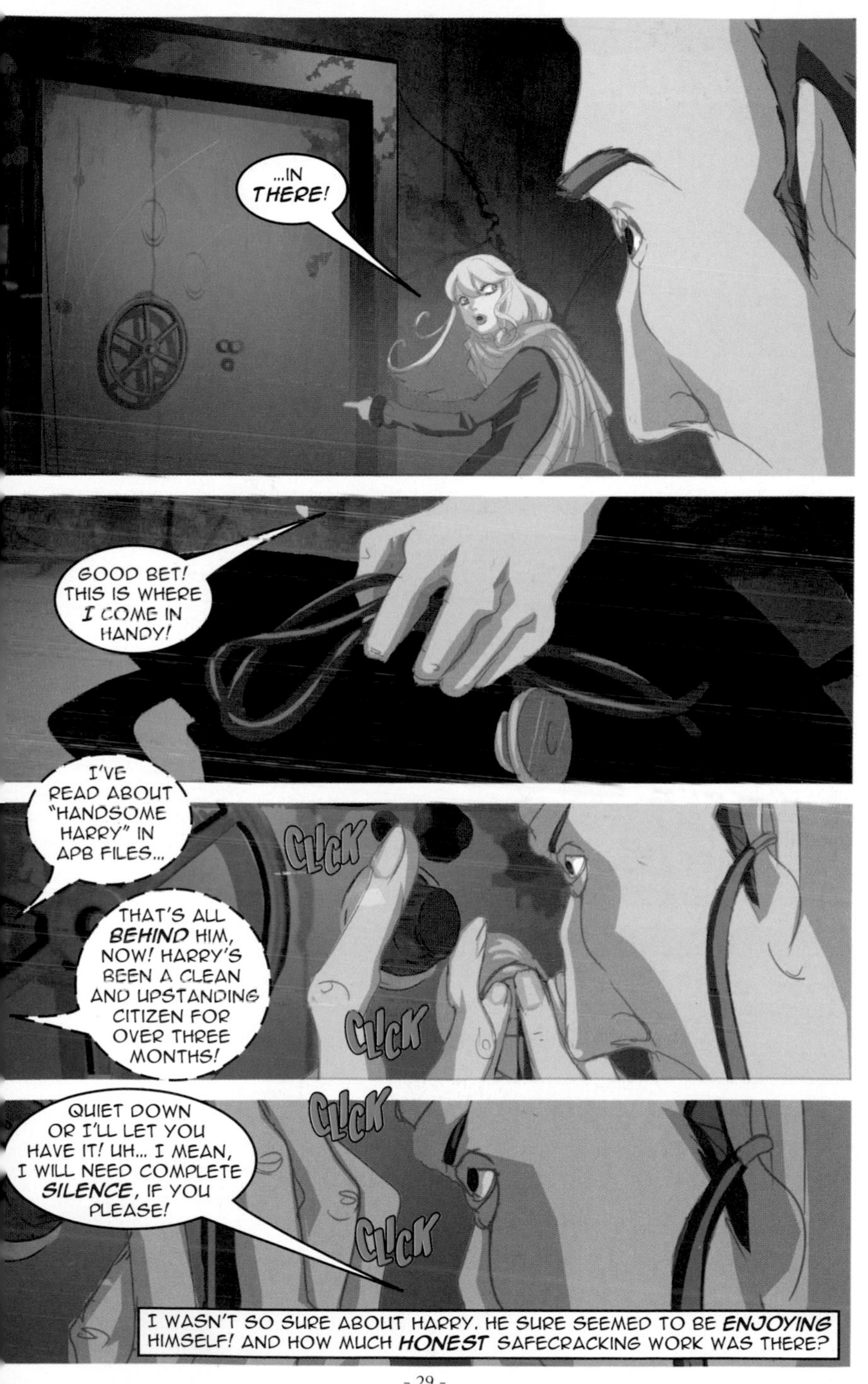
...IN THERE!
GOOD BET! THIS IS WHERE I COME IN HANDY!
I'VE READ ABOUT "HANDSOME HARRY" IN APB FILES...
CLICK
THAT'S ALL BEHIND HIM, NOW! HARRY'S BEEN A CLEAN AND UPSTANDING CITIZEN FOR OVER THREE MONTHS!
CLICK
QUIET DOWN OR I'LL LET YOU HAVE IT! UH... I MEAN, I WILL NEED COMPLETE SILENCE, IF YOU PLEASE!
CLICK
CLICK
I WASN'T SO SURE ABOUT HARRY. HE SURE SEEMED TO BE ENJOYING HIMSELF! AND HOW MUCH HONEST SAFECRACKING WORK WAS THERE?

REMEMBER HOW I SAID A MYSTERY ALWAYS DISTRACTS ME? YOU WOULD HAVE THOUGHT WITH THE ROOM SO QUIET...

...I'D HAVE HEARD SOMETHING MOVING IN THE ROOM...

BUT, I WAS SO ENGROSSED IN WONDERING WHAT WAS BEYOND THAT DOOR...

I WASN'T REALLY PAYING ATTENTION TO WHAT WAS RIGHT BEHIND ME. NOT UNTIL IT STARTED GETTING LOUD...
RRRUUUMMBBLLE
YOU HEAR SOME-THING?
YES, I DO!
RRRRUUMMMMBBBBLLE
RUUUMMMMBLLLLE
HEY, GUYS--
CAN'T YOU PLEASE BE-- ?

–QUIET?!
RUUUMMMMBLLLLLL
END CHAPTER ONE.

I'VE BEEN ACCUSED OF BEING SO FOCUSED ON A MYSTERY...
HARRY! LOOK OUT!

I'VE IGNORED WHAT'S RIGHT IN FRONT OF ME...
WHAT THE--?!
RRRUUUMMBBLLE

SO I COULD APPRECIATE HOW INTENSE HARRY WAS ABOUT HIS WORK.
RRRUUUMMBBLLE

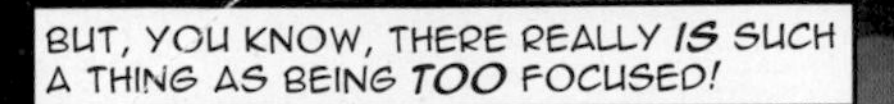

BUT, YOU KNOW, THERE REALLY IS SUCH A THING AS BEING TOO FOCUSED!
CRAAASHHHH

CHAPTER TWO: A CERTAIN MAGNETIC APPEAL

I DIDN'T REALIZE, UNTIL I SAW WHAT WAS LEFT, THAT THE CARRIER WAS LOADED WITH A FULL-SIZED TANK!

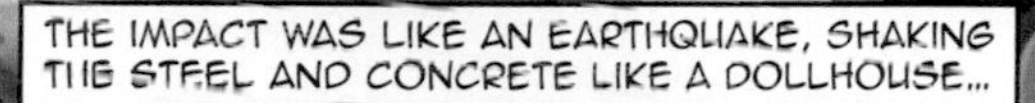

THE IMPACT WAS LIKE AN EARTHQUAKE, SHAKING THE STEEL AND CONCRETE LIKE A DOLLHOUSE...

...AND US LIKE DOLLS!
IT WAS THE SECOND TIME THAT NIGHT WE LOOKED DONE FOR!

BUT, LOOKS CAN BE DECEIVING AND I FOR ONE HAVE ALWAYS FOUND IT EASIER TO IGNORE MY LITTLE ACHES AND PAINS...
...WHEN THERE'S A MYSTERY TO SOLVE.
HA! HA! HA!
SO I GUESS BEING FOCUSED REALLY IS A TWO-EDGED SWORD, MEANING IT CAN BE BOTH BAD AND GOOD, A BOON AND A BANE!
A-HA! HA! HA!

FUNNY AND, WELL, NOT SAD, BUT KIND OF WEIRD!
HEY, I'M GLAD TO BE ALIVE, BUT I DON'T THINK IT'S ALL THAT HYSTERICAL.
HA! HA! NO, NO, NO! THE GHOST DID US A FAVOR!

YOU SEE?!
HE WAS RIGHT. IT WAS FUNNY, ONLY I WASN'T LAUGHING BECAUSE I WAS TOO AMAZED!
HUGE PIECES OF THE CARRIER WERE CLINGING TO THE WALL OF THE VAULT!
UNGH! QUITE STUCK, I'D SAY!
BUT, WHAT DOES IT MEAN, ASIDE FROM A HANDY WAY TO DO CHIN-UPS?!
UNGH! IT MEANS WE'VE FOUND THE TANK! IT MUST BE INSIDE THIS VAULT!

FAVOR? GUESS AGAIN! THE LOCK IS CRUSHED! I'LL NEED *POWER* DRILLS.
WE'LL HAVE TO GO GET THE GEN-ERATOR!
WE CAN'T! IT'S GETTING NEAR DAWN! WE DON'T HAVE MUCH TIME!
NONSENSE! THERE'S *PLENTY* OF TIME FOR ME TO FETCH THE EQUIPMENT.
AND FOR *ME* TO INVESTIGATE THE GHOST!

NOW, IF I CAN ONLY REMEMBER HOW TO PUT THIS THING TOGETHER...
LOOKS PRETTY *EASY*, WANT A HAND?
GENERATOR
WELL, WE CERTAINLY HAD A BIT OF LUCK RESCUING YOU GIRLS! MOST DAMSELS IN DISTRESS AREN'T NEARLY SO RESOURCEFUL!
SLAP
OW.
YEAH, BUT, NOT SO MUCH WITH THE FINDING OF *CLUES*.
WAIT! HERE'S SOMETHING! NOT VERY GHOSTLY, THOUGH.

OR SO I THOUGHT!
WHOA!
WHIZZ!
GHOST?
NOPE. MAGNET.

TELL ME ABOUT IT! THE GENERATOR WON'T EVEN RUN NEAR THAT BIG PAIN IN THE YOU-KNOW-WHAT!
HMPH! I'M NOT OUT OF TRICKS, YET!

AND THERE WAS HARRY WITH THAT FOCUS AGAIN!
THIS HOT-SHOT NON-MAGNETIC CHROMIUM MANGANESE AUSTENITIC STEEL LOCK MAY HAVE BEEN AHEAD OF ITS TIME IN WWII, BUT THAT'S BECAUSE IT NEVER MET UP WITH A LITTLE CORROSIVE ACID I LIKE TO CALL...

BERTHA BUBBLES!
IT IS ALWAYS NICE WHEN YOU CAN ENJOY YOUR WORK.

AND THE FUN WAS JUST BEGINNING...
GOOOO!
THIS IS ONE GHOST THAT JUST WOULDN'T QUIT!
GEEEET OOOUUUT!
BUT I GUESS THAT'S HOW YOU GET TO BE A GHOST IN THE FIRST PLACE!
ERK!
I HAD LOTS OF QUESTIONS FOR THIS "GHOST." IN LIEU OF A SÉANCE, I OPTED FOR THE MORE *DIRECT* APPROACH.

NO! THIS PLACE MUST REMAIN SECRET FOREVER!
HE SHOULDN'T HAVE SAID THAT! FOREVER AND SECRET ARE TWO WORDS THAT DON'T GO TOGETHER IN MY BOOK!

EVEN IF I HAVE TO KILL YOU ALL!
BERTHA BUBBLES! NO!

YEEOOWW!

YOU... MUST... NEVER... KNOW...
FUNNY, I DIDN'T THINK PAIN WOULD BE A BIG PROBLEM FOR GHOSTS.
WHAT HAPPENED?! DID HE GET ACID ON HIM?!
NO. THE BOTTLE IS STILL SEALED.

HE FORGOT HIS FLASHLIGHT. WE'D BETTER GO RETURN IT.
YOU MEAN NOW?
WHY FIGHT IT?! BESIDES, NOW WE KNOW IT ISN'T A REAL GHOST!
YEAH, BUT HE STILL LOOKED REAL MAD!

I WAS A LITTLE WORRIED ABOUT THIS GHOST HUNT MYSELF, ESPECIALLY NOW THAT I KNEW IT WAS A *LIVE* CRAZY MAN.
BUT, YOU KNOW, I WOULD NEVER HAVE SOLVED A *SINGLE* MYSTERY IF IT WASN'T FOR SOMETHING ELEANOR ROOSEVELT SAID.
WE HAVE TO LOOK FEAR IN THE FACE.

SO THAT'S WHAT I TRY TO DO, EVEN IF THE FACE OF FEAR IS SOMETIMES, YOU KNOW, ***SCARY!***

LIKE WHEN YOU'RE STARING AT A TON OF ***EXPLOSIVES*** SET TO BLOW UP THE BUILDING YOU'RE STANDING IN!

YOU CERTAINLY TAKE US TO SOME INTERESTING PLACES, NANCY!

YEAH, NEXT OUTING, I'M PLANNING! MAYBE A NICE BOTTLE-CAP FACTORY THAT HAS ***TOURS*** SCHEDULED INSTEAD OF ***DEMO-LITIONS!***

MEANWHILE, THE MEN WERE BUSY WITH BERTHA...
MAYBE WE SHOULD FORGET THIS AND GO HELP THE GIRLS!
NO! WE MUST REACH THE TANK WHILE THERE'S TIME! BESIDES, SOMETHING TELLS ME NANCY DREW CAN HANDLE HERSELF!
TRY NOT TO BREATHE!
COUGH COUGH NO KIDDING.

MEANWHILE, ABOUT THE ONLY THING I DISCOVERED ABOUT THE GHOST WAS THAT HE WASN'T AFRAID OF **HEIGHTS**!

PART OF ME WANTED TO WALK UP AND **KNOCK**, BUT I DIDN'T KNOW **WHAT** THIS GUY WAS CAPABLE OF, AND I COULDN'T PUT MY FRIENDS IN THAT KIND OF DANGER.

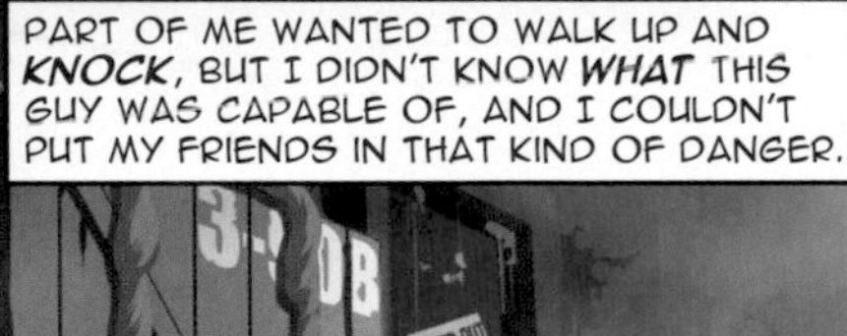
KEEP OUT

CHEERING FROM BELOW TOLD US THAT BERTHA HAD DONE THE JOB!
YAY!

BUT THERE GOES THAT FOCUS THING AGAIN! SOMETIMES YOU CAN'T TAKE YOUR EYES OFF THE PRIZE FOR A SECOND!
DUCK!
THESE SECRETS ARE FOREVER! MUST STOP THEM....
HAD HE HEARD US?
MMPH!
3-908

IF HE DID, HE WAS PROBABLY TOO USED TO THE SOUND OF ALL THE RATS TO PAY ANY MIND!
3 90B

HE'S GONE. LET'S GO.
IN *THERE*?! SHOULDN'T WE GO AFTER *HIM*?!

LET'S SEE, CRAZY GUY WITH KNIFE, OR CREEPY ROOM!
TOUGH CHOICE, HUH?

BEFORE I WALKED IN THAT ROOM, I THOUGHT OBSESSIVELY *CLEAN* PEOPLE WERE A LITTLE CRAZY, TOO...

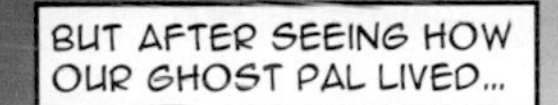

BUT AFTER SEEING HOW OUR GHOST PAL LIVED...

...I DECIDED THAT CLEAN IS DEFINITELY BETTER!

AT LEAST HE'S EATING RIGHT.
YOU KNOW, SOME SCIENTISTS SUSPECT EATING OUT OF ALUMINUM CAN GIVE YOU ALZHEIMER'S. MAYBE THAT'S WHY HE'S SO CRANKY.
COOL. BUT, WITHOUT ELECTRICITY, HE *CAN'T* BE GETTING GREAT RECEPTION.

THESE PHOTOS SHOW THIS FACTORY BACK WHEN IT WAS UP AND RUNNING.

HELLO, WHAT'S THIS?
SIX SAVED BY NIGHT WATCHMAN
AT RIVER HEIGHTS MUNITIONS FACTORY
IT'S OUR GHOST AS A YOUNG MAN! HE EVEN HAS THE SAME HELMET!
LOOKS LIKE HE WAS SOME KIND OF HERO!
HEY, CHECK THIS OUT!

THIS PRESCRIPTION MEDICINE IS ONLY A FEW DAYS OLD. THAT COINCIDES WITH THE DATE THE MYSTERIOUS LIGHT WAS FIRST SPOTTED.
NANCE...

NANCY!
WHAT?
REMEMBER HOW I'VE BEEN TALKING ABOUT FOCUS? TURNS OUT SOMETIMES, YOU HAVE TO PAY CLOSE ATTENTION TO EVERYTHING!

GH-GH-GHOOST... H-H-HOME... N-N-NOW...
I HADN'T EVEN HEARD HIM, WHICH WAS SURPRISING WITH ALL THE MUTTERING HE'D BEEN DOING EARLIER.
HE LOOKS SURPRISED FOR A MINUTE. I WASN'T SURE *WHAT* I COULD SAY TO APPEASE HIM.
UNFORTUNATELY, I FAILED TO COME UP WITH ANYTHING INTELLIGENT.
UH... HI?

THAT'S IT!
WE'RE IN!

WHILE WE WERE BEING CORNERED, THE MEN USED ALL THE STRENGTH THEY COULD MUSTER TO GET TO THEIR BOOTY.

AND THEY FINALLY HAD THEIR EYES ON *THEIR* PRIZE!

YAHOO!
THERE'S THE TANK, MR. CREDO! WE DID IT!
YES. I SUPPOSE WE DID.

I'LL SHOW YOU TO MESS WITH ME AND MY STUFF.
WAIT YOU DON'T HAVE TO...

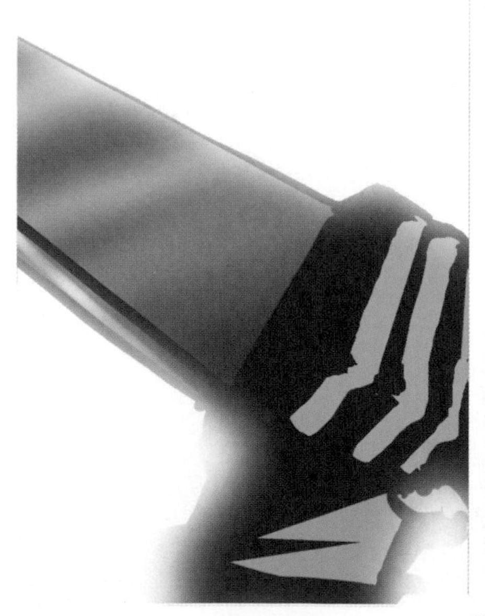
IT WAS JUST THEN, I FINALLY FIGURED OUT EXACTLY WHAT I WANTED TO SAY TO HIM!

BUT IT WAS TOO LATE!
END CHAPTER TWO

IT WAS ONE OF THOSE SECONDS THAT SEEMS TO HAPPEN IN SLOW MOTION. WHILE YOU WISH IT WOULD *END*...
...IT LASTS *FOREVER!*

TURNS OUT THE OPEN TANK *VAULT* WAS MAKING ANY METAL IN THE WHOLE PLACE PULL TOWARD THE TANK...

CLANG

MAGNETIZING ANY METAL WALLS.

GUESS I'M JUST *LUCKY* THAT WAY!

CHAPTER THREE: TANKS FOR THE MEMORIES!

OUR STRANGE GHOST-FRIEND... NOT SO LUCKY.
YEEOOWW!
BUT I WAS STARTING TO FIGURE OUT EXACTLY WHAT HIS PROBLEM WAS.
NO! THEY FOUND IT! NO! MY HEAD!
MUST STOP THEM...
WAIT!

WE SHOULD FOLLOW HIM.
BUT, BUT...I'M SO HAPPY HE'S LEAVING!
HE'S IN SOME KIND OF PAIN!
OKAY! SO, HE'S HUMAN ENOUGH! BUT, HELPING HIM MIGHT BE LIKE TRYING TO PET A RATTLE-SNAKE!
GONE! HE'S NO GHOST, BUT HE SURE HAS A GHOST'S PENCHANT FOR VANISHING!
LET'S JUST GO BACK TO THE TANK, WHERE IT'S UH, SAFER!
YEAH. I HAVE A FEELING WE HAVEN'T SEEN THE LAST OF THAT CREEP-KEEPER! AND IT'S NOT A FEELING I ENJOY.

BACK AT THE TANK, THINGS WEREN'T MUCH CHEERIER.
YOU MUST GET THIS THING RUNNING, HARRY!
OPEN YOUR EYES! THERE'S NO WAY TO WORK ON THIS ENGINE WITH METAL TOOLS!
HEY, YOU'RE BACK!
HMM... I'LL BET THERE'S SOME WAY TO IMPROVISE!
EVEN IF WE COULD FIGURE OUT HOW TO WORK ON IT, WE WOULDN'T HAVE TIME! THEY'RE GOING TO LEVEL THIS PLACE IN THIRTY MINUTES!
IN FIFTEEN MINUTES WE'LL HAVE TO BAG THE TANK AND SAVE OUR OWN SKINS, BUT MEAN-WHILE, IS THERE ANY HOPE FOR GETTING IT OUT ALIVE?
I'LL SEE WHAT I CAN DO!
THANK GOODNESS ONE OF US COULD AFFORD A WATCH WITH ELINVAR HAIRSPRINGS, OR WE WOULDN'T EVEN KNOW WHAT TIME IT WAS!
WELL YOU DON'T HAVE TO BE RICH TO CARRY A HAIR SCRUNCHIE OR A PLASTIC CUTICLE PUSHER.
IN CASE YOU'RE CURIOUS, ELINVAR IS A SPECIAL ALLOY THAT'S NON-MAGNETIC. THE NAME IS SHORT FOR ELASTICALLY INVARIABLE.

GREAT HERA, IT'S ON!
WELL, I TURNED IT ON! BUT, I STILL HAVE SOME TINKERING TO DO TO GET THE ENGINE RUNNING!
YOU'RE JUST FULL OF SURPRISES, AREN'T YOU?
WELL, BESS'S MECHANICAL KNACK IS NO SURPRISE TO GEORGE AND ME.
PLEASE, MY DEAR! DON'T PAUSE! I KNOW YOU CAN GET THIS OLD MONSTROSITY FIRED UP FOR BATTLE BEFORE THE ENEMY ATTACKS!
UH, SIR, YES SIR?

IN ALL THE EXCITEMENT OF OUR COUNTDOWN TO DESTRUCTION I'D ALMOST FORGOTTEN ABOUT OUR POOR DEMENTED GHOST MAN.
OOOOWWWW!
I COULDN'T BE SURE HE KNEW ABOUT THE DEMOLITION PLAN AND I DIDN'T HAVE MUCH TIME TO WARN HIM.
RATHER THAN DISTRACT ANYONE FROM THE TANK'S LIBERATION...
I FIGURED I'D HANDLE THIS MYSELF.
MOOAAN
ONLY TO DISCOVER I WASN'T THE ONLY ONE TAKING MATTERS INTO MY OWN HANDS.
WHAT ARE YOU DOING?!

PLEASE, STOP... FELIX!
YOU! HOW DO YOU KNOW MY NAME?!
I READ THE ARTICLE ABOUT YOU IN YOUR ROOM! YOU'RE QUITE A HERO, AREN'T YOU, FELIX?
YOU'RE AN ENEMY AGENT, A SPY!
NO, FELIX.
THE WAR ENDED IN 1945. THE ENEMY WAS DEFEATED OVER SIXTY YEARS AGO.
STOP! YOU'VE BEEN TRAINED TO CONFUSE ME!

IT'S NOT ME. IT'S THAT METAL PLATE IN YOUR HEAD THAT'S CONFUSING YOU...
...THE ONE YOU GOT AFTER YOU WERE INJURED, SAVING THIS PLANT FROM A REAL SPY!
I FOUND A BOMB! THERE WERE STILL SOME TECHNICIANS IN THE BUILDING -- WORKING LATE.
I WARNED THEM, THEN CAME BACK TO MAKE SURE NO ONE GOT LEFT BEHIND... AND THE TANK WAS SAFE. IT HAD TO BE KEPT SECRET!
"BUT THE BOMB WENT OFF BEFORE I COULD DISCONNECT ALL THE DYNAMITE!
"I WAS SICK FOR A LONG TIME. BUT, THEY KEPT PROMISING TO SEND ME BACK TO MY POST, HERE AT THE PLANT."
BUT WHEN THIS PLANT CLOSED, THERE WAS NO JOB TO GO BACK TO. YOU SPENT MOST OF YOUR LIFE IN A VETERAN'S HOSPITAL SINCE THE INJURY AFFECTED YOUR MIND.

"WHEN THEY FINALLY RELEASED ME A FEW *MONTHS* AGO. I CAME BACK HERE JUST TO *SEE* THE PLACE.
"WHEN I FOUND *NO ONE* HERE, I REALIZED THEY WERE ENTRUSTING THE PLANT'S SECURITY TO *ME!*"
FELIX, LISTEN.
WHEN YOU CAME BACK, THE MAGNETS AFFECTED THE METAL PLATE IN YOUR HEAD. YOU BECAME DELUSIONAL, BELIEVING YOU STILL HAD TO PROTECT THE BASE, BUT YOU *DON'T* AND *CAN'T*.
WE'LL GET YOU SOME *HELP!* BUT, WE HAVE TO GET OUT OF HERE, *NOW!*
NO! YOU'RE *LYING!* I CAN'T LET YOU GET AWAY WITH THE *PRECIOUS* SECRETS!
FELIX, *NO!*

WHAT WAS THAT?! YOU HEAR SOME-THING?
NO.
HEH! SURPRISINGLY, NOT A BAD LOOK.
ONLY BESS COULD MAKE GREASE LOOK GOOD.
ALMOST DONE. GEORGE, I NEED YOUR PLASTIC COMB TO DO ONE MORE THING.
OKAY. BUT, I'LL NEED IT BACK. MUST LOOK MY BEST FOR BLOWING UP.
SIMMER DOWN! WITH ANY LUCK WE'LL BE OUT BEFORE ANYTHING EXPLODES.

I WASN'T SO SURE!
OOMPH!
GOTCHA!
FFFFTT

THESE ARE THE AWKWARD MOMENTS I LIVE FOR!
PHEW! TOO CLOSE FOR MY TASTE, FELIX.
YOU ARE A SPY! I KNEW IT!

I LET MY GUARD DOWN. I MUST NEVER-- ARRRGH!
I REALLY WANTED TO HELP THIS GUY, BUT I WAS STARTING TO WISH IT WERE AS EASY AS PETTING A RATTLESNAKE!
YEEEIIII!
AS THE SUN CAME UP, EVERYTHING WENT BLACK...
...AGAIN.
MATA HARI... MUTTER... CAN'T LET THEM TAKE SECRETS... MUTTER.

HEY THERE, EAST END. -SQUAWK- WE ARE IN POSITION -SQUAWK- AT THE WEST END OF BUILDING, OVER.
ROGER, THAT. WE'RE ALL SET HERE AT THE ENTRANCE. THE EXPLOSIVES LAID YESTERDAY JUST NEED TO HAVE DETONATORS CONNECTED AND THEY'LL BE GOOD TO GO OR SHOULD I SAY **BLOW**?! OVER.
SHOULD I DO THE FINAL CLEAR-- MAKE SURE THE PLACE IS **EMPTY**?
YUP!
GRAB A **BULLHORN** AND WARN THE MICE AND PIGEONS THAT THEY'VE GOTTA **RELOCATE**.
JUST TELL 'EM NOT TO COME TO **MY** HOUSE, WILL YA?

TIME'S UP, GREASE MONKEY! LOOKS LIKE WE'RE GOING TO HAVE TO GIVE UP AND LEAVE THE THING *HERE*.
HEY, ***WHERE'S*** OUR GIRL DETECTIVE?!
YOU MEAN YOUR FELLOW *SPY*?!

AAARGH! YOU FILTHY SPIES THOUGHT YOU'D WALTZ OUT WITH MILITARY SECRETS, BUT ***NO ONE*** IS LEAVING HERE.
NO ONE!
CLANG

THE GHOST MAY BE RIGHT! THIS THING ISN'T BUDGING.
HE MUST HAVE RIGGED THE BALLAST TO BREAK ON CLOSING!
DEMOLITION IS SCHEDULED FOR SEVEN! IT'S FIVE TO. THEY'RE PROBABLY OUTSIDE NOW, GETTING READY.
THEY'LL HAVE TO CHECK THE PLACE FOR SQUATTERS FIRST!
YARRGH! WE'LL ALL DIE TOGETHER! UNNGH! 'TIS A FAR, FAR BETTER THING I DO...

FIRST LET'S SHUT THIS GUY UP.
AT LEAST KEEP HIM STILL.
NOOO!
CLANG
WELL, I WOULD DIAL 911, BUT THE CELL IS USELESS BECAUSE OF THE MAGNETIC FIELD.

ANYONE IN THE BUILDING, PLEASE EVACUATE IMMEDIATELY! I REPEAT, YOU HAVE THREE MINUTES TO EVACUATE.
BEEP BEEP BEEP
VROOMMMM

03:00
CLICK
CLICK
CLICK

HELLOOO! WE'RE HERE! WE'RE HERE!
UH, GUYS...
VROOOOM-M

BRRRRAAAAAAAAAAAAANNNN
SLAM
...I KNOW WE'RE ALL GOING TO DIE, BUT THE GOOD NEWS IS... I GOT THE TANK RUNNING.
EVERYONE IN THE TANK, NOW!
WAIT, SHOULDN'T YOU DRIVE, BESS?!
NO TIME FOR SWITCHING SEATS IN THIS TIGHT SQUEEZE! JUST PRESS BOTH THOSE PEDALS TO THE METAL, NOW!

WE FORGOT AND ALMOST KILLED THE GHOST!
OH, MY GOD! FELIX!
WHO?!
VRRMMMM
CRASH
YEEIIIII!
CLANK
=UPP!= NOT TO WORRY! HE'LL BE JOINING US AFTER ALL!

SORRY! BESS, WHERE'S THE STEERING WHEEL?!
THOSE ARE THE BRAKES! USE THEM TO STEER.
GENTLY PULL BACK ONE OR THE OTHER TO TURN. PULL HARD ON BOTH TO STOP!
GOT IT!
WHOOOAA! SHE SAID GENTLY! MAYBE YOU SHOULD PLAY MORE TANK COMMANDER!
SORRY!

OKAY! I THINK I'M GETTING THE HANG OF IT!
IS FELIX STILL HANGING ON!
YEEIIIII!
THAT WOULD BE A "YES!"
I SUGGEST HEADING IN THE DIRECTION OF THAT BIG DOOR!

02:20
HUMMMM
AFTER A FEW PRACTICE CIRCLES PROVED ME A LOUSY TANK DRIVER, I MANAGED TO AIM THE THING AT THE DOOR. BUT, I WAS CONCERNED ROY AND FELIX WOULD BE INJURED AS WE RIPPED THROUGH IT AND WHATEVER WALLS WERE BETWEEN US AND FREEDOM.
DON'T WORRY ABOUT A FEW BUMPS OR BRUISES! IF YOU DON'T GET US THROUGH THAT DOOR NOW, WE'LL ALL BE BLOWN TO PIECES! I SUSPECT THAT WOULD BE WORSE.
HMMMMM
00:40

OKAY! HANG ON! WE'RE GOING *THROUGH*.

HEEEYAAAA!
VRRRROOOMMMM

YEEHHAAH!
NOOOOO!
YAAAHHOOO!
VRRRROOOMMMM

00:1
CRASH
00:17
CRASH

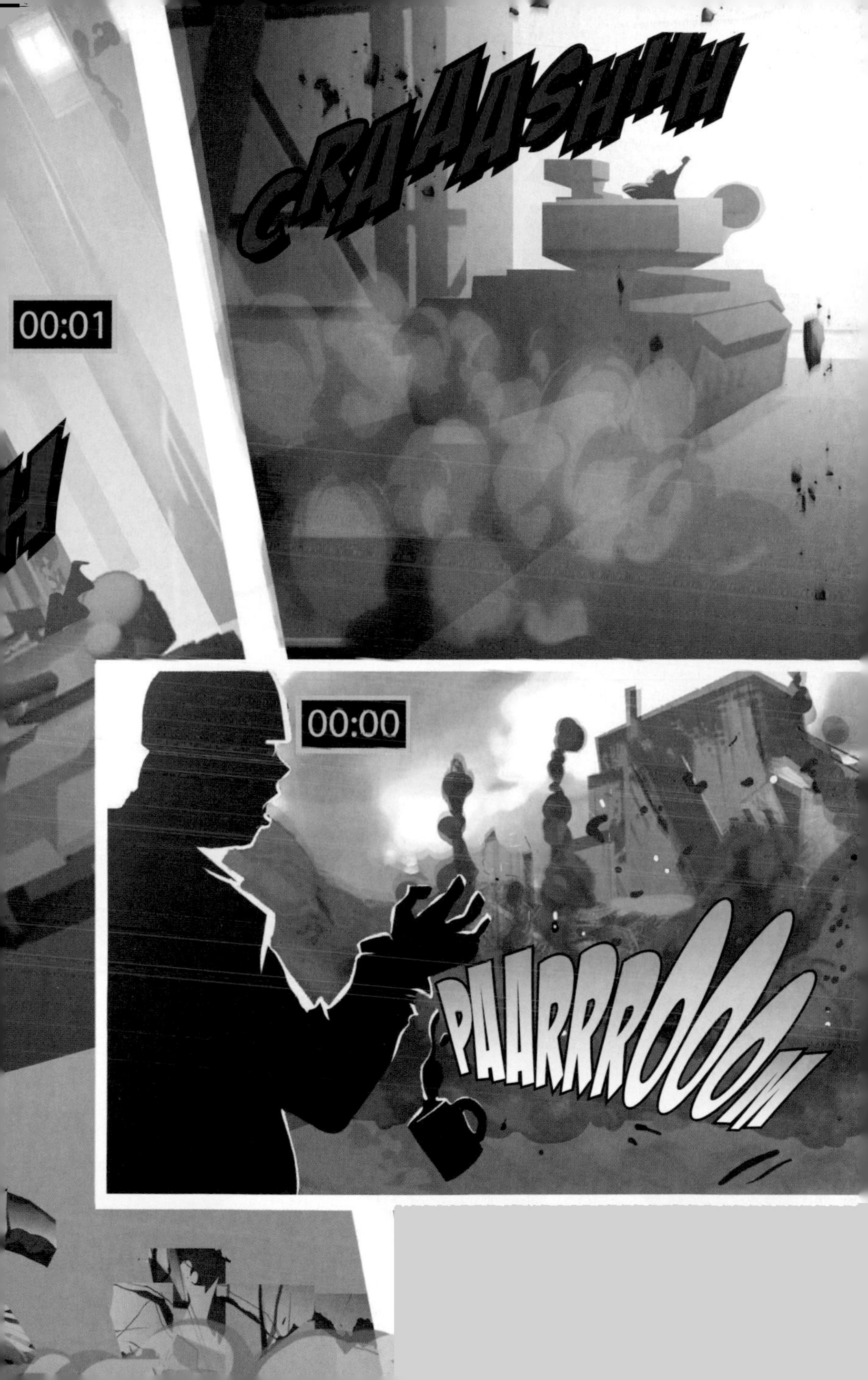
CRAAASHHH
00:01
00:00
PAARRROOOM

WHAT THE --?!
SCREEEECH
PRRRRMMMMMM
HELLO! NANCY DREW HERE, GIRL DETECTIVE!
H-HELLO.
GOOD HEAVENS?! IS HE ALL RIGHT?!
HARD TO SAY! BETTER CALL AN AMBULANCE FOR OUR HERO.

YOU'RE THE HERO, NANCY, GETTING US ALL OUT ALIVE!
AND USING YOUR HEAD SO... WELL, LITERALLY.
ALL IN A DAY'S WORK! I'M NOT LOOKING FOR ANY MEDALS.
KNOCKED OUT THREE TIMES, EH? WELL, NO CONCUSSION, AND NO PURPLE HEART! YOU'LL BE FINE.
THEN ALLOW ME TO SHOW MY GRATITUDE BY SAYING, TANKS!
OHHHH!
PLEASE!
SO, CAN WE GET A LIFT BACK TO TOWN?!
YOU GO AHEAD. I'M GOING TO TAKE A LONG SLOW WALK!
WAS IT MY JOKES?! WHAT?!
THE END

WATCH OUT FOR PAPERCUTZ

Hi, mystery-lovers! Welcome to the fifth double-dose of NANCY DREW DIARIES from Papercutz, those armchair detectives dedicated to publishing great graphic novels for all ages. I'm Jim Salicrup, the Editor-in-Chief and honorary Teen Sleuth.

NEW STORY! FULL-COLOR GRAPHIC NOVEL
NANCY DREW
girl detective
#11
MONKEY WRENCH BLUES
BASED ON THE SERIES BY CAROLYN KEENE
PETRUCHA & KINNEY
MURASE & GUZMAN
PAPERCUTZ

The two mysteries featured in this volume of NANCY DREW DIARIES are actually the first two parts of the three-part "The High Miles Mystery." As you can tell, each part was designed to stand on its own, but read together you get to see the bigger story. We wish we could've included the third part, but rest assured it's coming your way shortly! Of course if you really can't wait for the thrilling conclusion, you can order NANCY DREW GIRL DETECTIVE #11 "Monkey Wrench Blues" – use the same ordering info found at the bottom of page 175, and have it sent directly to your home. NANCY DREW DIARIES is, after all, re-presenting those stories, two at a time, in this series for the folks that might've missed out or been too young the first time they were published. And if you really, really can't wait for Part Three of "The High Miles Mystery," you can also order the e-book version of NANCY DREW GIRL DETECTIVE #11 and have it delivered to your favorite device instantly!

One of the other interesting facts about "The High Miles Mystery" is that it's the story where we finally started crediting Stefan's co-writer Sarah Kinney. Turned out that Sarah was helping Stefan write NANCY DREW graphic novels for some time, and we finally decided to make it official and give her the credit she so richly deserves. Some of you may remember Sarah from her writing the NANCY DREW AND THE CLUE CREW graphic novels also from Papercutz (Go to papercutz.com for more information). She's certainly has been a big part of all the NANCY DREW graphic novels from Papercutz for some time, and we just want to take this opportunity to applaud her for all her great work writing America's favorite Girl Detective!

Hey, thinking back to these early NANCY DREW stories suddenly made us realize that it's our tenth anniversary! That's right, Papercutz, which began back in 2005 with the release of both NANCY DREW GIRL DETECTIVE Graphic Novel #1 and THE HARDY BOYS Graphic Novel #1 is celebrating a birthday—the big One-O! Wait til you see one of the ways we're commemorating our anniversary! We'll tell you all about in NANCY DREW DIARIES #6, speaking of which, you won't want to miss that either! In addition to the much-discussed concluding part of "The High Miles Mystery," there's also a fun little mystery entitled "Dress Reversal"! Be there or be square!

Thanks,

Jim

STAY IN TOUCH!

EMAIL:	salicrup@papercutz.com
WEB:	www.papercutz.com
TWITTER:	@papercutzgn
FACEBOOK:	PAPERCUTZGRAPHICNOVELS
REGULAR MAIL:	Papercutz, 160 Broadway, Suite 700, East Wing, New York, NY 10038

NANCY DREW HERE, BOARDING MILLIONAIRE, RALPH CREDO'S ***PRIVATE CHOO-CHOO*** WITH ITS SPECIAL NEW ***WOODEN*** CARGO CAR.

IT HAD TO BE ***WOODEN*** TO CARRY AN EXPERIMENTAL TANK DEVELOPED DURING WORLD WAR II, A TANK I RECENTLY DROVE OUT OF AN OLD MUNITIONS PLANT JUST BEFORE IT ***BLEW UP!***

THE ENGINE USES THESE ***DANGEROUSLY*** POWERFUL MAGNETS TO INCREASE ITS GAS MILEAGE A HUNDRED-FOLD.

IT WAS BEING BROUGHT TO MR. CREDO'S RESEARCH FACILITY WHERE THE SCIENTIST ROY HINKLEY WANTED TO UNLOCK ITS SECRETS TO REVOLUTIONIZE THE CAR INDUSTRY!

ROY AND RALPH WERE SO ***GRATEFUL*** FOR MY HELP THAT THEY INVITED ME AND MY FRIENDS ALONG FOR THE TRIP! AND WHAT GIRL DETECTIVE COULD RESIST?

CHAPTER ONE: TICKET TO HIDE

MY HEAD ACQUIRED A FEW EXTRA LUMPS AT THE PLANT, TOO.
I SUSPECT THAT'S WHY MY BOYFRIEND NED THOUGHT HE'D BETTER JOIN US FOR THE RIDE....
since 1920
ROY, THIS IS NED.
NICE TO MEET YOU, SON! ANY FRIEND OF NANCY'S IS A FRIEND OF MINE! OUR GAL REALLY TAKES A LICKING AND KEEPS ON TICKING, DOESN'T SHE?
I HEARD SHE'S BEEN A LITTLE ACCIDENT-PRONE, SO I'M HERE TO MAKE SURE SHE, UH...
...WEARS THIS!
AH HA! VALOROUS INDEED, MY YOUNG FRIEND! VALOROUS INDEED.
VERY FUNNY.

YEAH, LIKE THAT HELMET WILL KEEP YOU OUT OF TROUBLE FOR MORE THAN A MINUTE OR TWO.
NOW THERE'S A CHALLENGE INDEED! BUT, WITHOUT YOU INTREPID GIRLS, THIS WONDERFUL TANK WOULD BE UNDER A PILE OF RUBBLE RIGHT NOW.
ALONG WITH OUR CARCASSES!
G1
River Heights
I'M JUST GLAD MY PART IN THIS ADVENTURE IS OVER. YOU CAN KEEP YOUR JAMES BOND EXCITEMENT.
JUST PAY ME AND DROP ME OFF AT THE NEAREST TOWN. SOMEPLACE SAFE AND QUIET, LIKE MANHATTAN!
MR. HARRY SHARRY IS A REFORMED SAFECRACKER WHO HELPED FIND THE TANK. HE SEEMS GRUFF, BUT, WE ALL GET CRANKY IF WE DON'T SLEEP FOR A COUPLE OF DAYS.

YOU'LL HAVE TO CONTENT YOURSELF WITH DENVER, MY FRIEND, WHERE CREDO INC. HAS THEIR RESEARCH FACILITY!
I'M GOING TO STUDY THAT ENGINE AND BUILD A MODEL STABLE ENOUGH FOR STREET VEHICLES!
WE'RE GOING TO REVOLUTIONIZE THE INDUSTRY, BROTHER! AND YOU CAN SAY YOU HELPED!
G1
ights
WHEN WE GET TO DENVER, RALPH WILL FLY YOU HOME! NOW, PERHAPS A NAP WILL IMPROVE YOUR DISPOSITION?
SLEEPING BERTHS TO THE REAR, SITTING AND DINING UP FRONT.
ALL ABOARD THE CREDO EXPRESS!
THANKS, MR. CREDO! YOU'RE VERY NICE TO LET US COME FOR THE RIDE.

I HATE TO THINK HOW MUCH THIS LITTLE PARTY OF YOURS WILL COST, MR. CREDO.
JOE BLANDER, MY ASSISTANT. I ACTUALLY PAY JOE TO NAG ME.
IT'S A PRIVATE TRAIN, JOE. IT COSTS AS MUCH TO CARRY TEN PEOPLE AS IT DOES TO CARRY FIVE.
FINE, BUT EVEN PRIVATE TRAINS HAVE TO LEAVE ON TIME AND YOUR LAWYER STILL ISN'T ON BOARD!
JOE'S ALL ABOUT THE TIME AND MONEY.
I JUST THINK, THE MORE THE MERRIER.

OH, DEAR, IT'S THE DEFECTIVE GIRL DETECTIVE AND HER RATTY PALS!
DEIRDRE! WHAT ARE YOU DOING HERE?
DADDY IS LEGAL COUNCIL TO CREDO INCORPORATED.
WHAT? REALLY?! UH... I GUESS. MR. SHANNON IS CERTAINLY, UH, SKILLED.
YOU MEAN RUTHLESS AND UNETHICAL!
I WAS WORRIED THE TRIP MIGHT BE DULL. I NEVER THOUGHT IT WOULD ACTUALLY BE PAINFUL...
WELL, THANKS FOR DISPROVING THE WHOLE "THE MORE THE MERRIER" THING!

NED?! YOU'RE HERE, TOO?!
I TAKE IT ALL BACK. DESPITE GEORGIA'S FORKED TONGUE, THIS MIGHT BE FUN AFTER ALL.
BAD MOVE. GEORGE DID NOT LIKE BEING CALLED GEORGIA!
WHY, DEEDEE? PLANNING TO THROW YOURSELF FROM THE TRAIN?
YOU TWO BETTER COOL IT AND FIND A SEAT!
I FIGURED I SHOULD SEPARATE THEM BEFORE A WAR BROKE OUT...
BUT FATE ACTUALLY THREW THEM TOGETHER!
YEEIKES!

SORRY ABOUT THAT!
THE TRAIN HAS ITS OWN POWERFUL ENGINE AND OUR ENGINEER LOVES TO SHOOT IT OUT OF THE STATION LIKE A BULLET.
ONCE WE'RE UP TO SPEED, YOU'LL BARELY NOTICE WE'RE MOVING.
MAJOR COOLNESS! IS THE ENGINE A CUSTOM DESIGN?
I SAW SOLAR PANELS OUTSIDE. IS IT ECO-FRIENDLY?
SIGH
YOU TWO WOULD BEG FOR A SCIENCE LESSON. MAYBE I WILL THROW MYSELF FROM THE TRAIN!

MY LITTLE TRAIN'S ONE OF A KIND. IT'S SAFE TO MOVE ABOUT, NOW. WOULD YOU LIKE A TOUR?
THANKS!
COUNT ME IN!
BEATS SITTING WITH DEEDEE!
WON'T YOU TWO JOIN US?
NO THANKS! NEDDY AND I CAN JUST SIT AND ENJOY EACH OTHER'S COMPANY!
UH, ACTUALLY, I HAVE TO FINISH THIS BOOK FOR CLASS. I HAVE ANOTHER I COULD LOAN YOU TO READ...
papercutz
Shakespeare
2nd Edition
NINA
UCHH. NO THANKS!
A TOUR OF A LUXURY TRAIN SUDDENLY ISN'T SOUNDING SO BAD.

NO ONE WAS SURPRISED THAT READING WASN'T DEIRDRE'S FAVORITE PASTIME. IN FACT, GEORGE WAS SURPRISED TO HEAR SHE KNEW HOW TO READ AT ALL, AND ***DISAPPOINTED*** THAT SHE JOINED US.

I DIDN'T MIND. I TRUSTED NED, BUT I KNEW SHE WOULD JUST WIND UP ANNOYING HIM.

MEANWHILE, I WAS ENJOYING THE SCENERY AND RALPH CREDO'S ENTHUSIASM ABOUT HIS COOL TRAIN.
BACK AT THE MUNITIONS FACTORY, HE SEEMED PRETTY UNEXCITED ABOUT THE TANK HE WAS THERE TO SAVE.
HERE HE WAS LIKE A KID SHOWING US HIS FAVORITE TOY.

THOSE BUFFALO AREN'T LIKELY TO STAMPEDE, ARE THEY?!
THIS SOLARIUM AND OBSERVATORY ARE PRESSURIZED FOR SAFETY AND COMFORT...
AND ALL THE WINDOWS GIVE YOU THE THRILL OF FEELING LIKE YOU'RE RIDING OUTSIDE THE TRAIN.
IT ALSO ACTS AS A BUFFER BETWEEN THE PASSENGER CAR AND THE ENGINE, WHICH IS THROUGH HERE.
GOOD. WE REALLY SHOULD KEEP POOR GEORGIA OUT OF THE SUN. SHE WOULDN'T WANT TO GET ANY MORE WRINKLED!
CONTROL ROOM
IT'S GEORGE, DEEDEE! GEORGE!

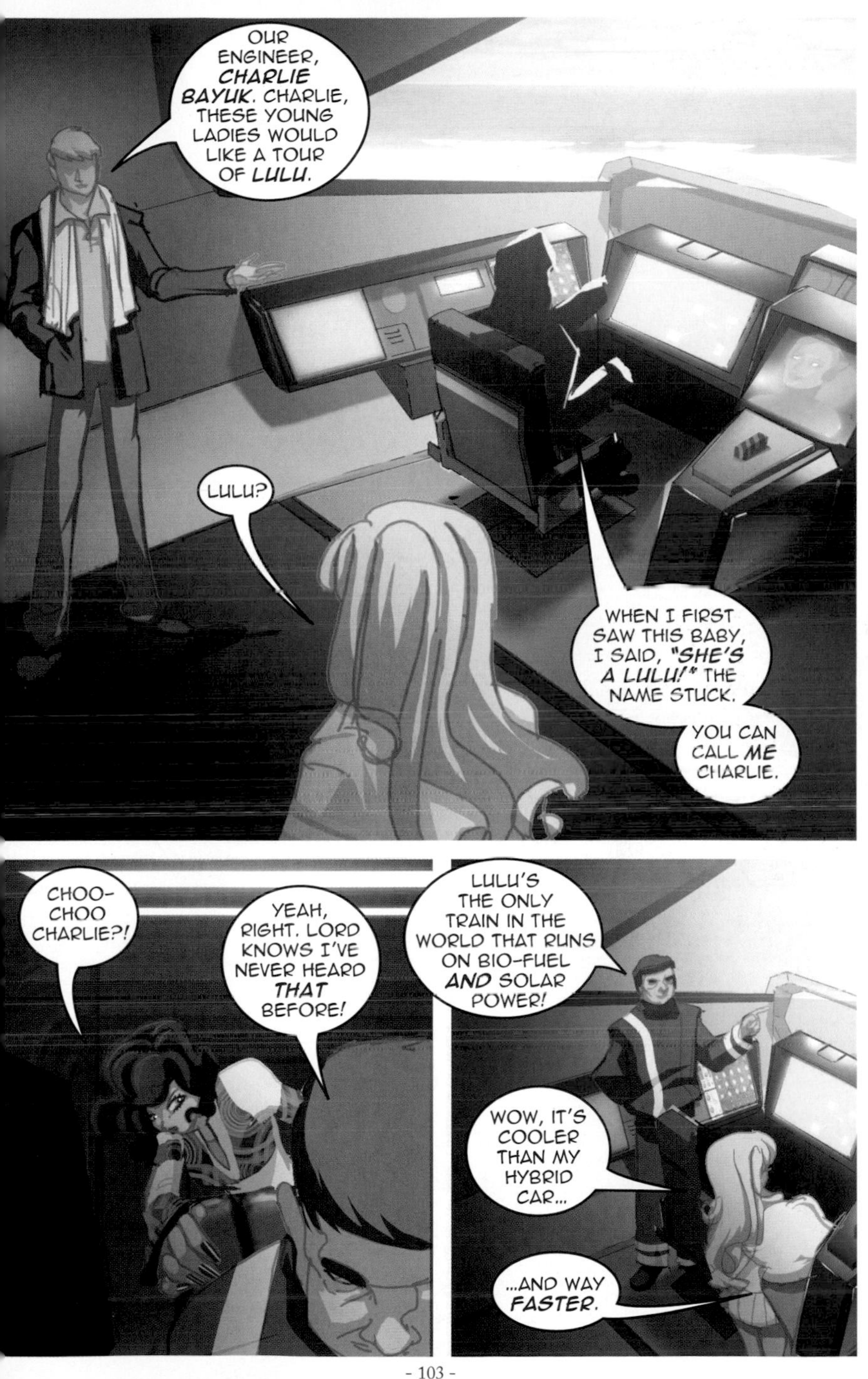
OUR ENGINEER, CHARLIE BAYUK. CHARLIE, THESE YOUNG LADIES WOULD LIKE A TOUR OF LULU.
LULU?
WHEN I FIRST SAW THIS BABY, I SAID, "SHE'S A LULU!" THE NAME STUCK.
YOU CAN CALL ME CHARLIE.
CHOO-CHOO CHARLIE?!
YEAH, RIGHT. LORD KNOWS I'VE NEVER HEARD THAT BEFORE!
LULU'S THE ONLY TRAIN IN THE WORLD THAT RUNS ON BIO-FUEL AND SOLAR POWER!
WOW, IT'S COOLER THAN MY HYBRID CAR...
...AND WAY FASTER.

-SIGH-
HEY! DON'T SIT ON THAT!
NO SWEAT! LULU'S GOT A COMPUTER OVER-RIDE FOR PILOTING, TO PREVENT ANY POSSIBLE HUMAN ERRORS.
THAT'S HANDY, IN CASE YOU GET DISTRACTED BY ALL THE BEAUTIFUL, UH...
...BUFFALO.
THE FACT WAS, OTHER THAN TINY ANIMALS, THERE WASN'T MUCH TO LOOK AT!

OH, IT'S NOT SO LONELY.
THE COMPUTER TALKS! CREDO INC. WAS KIND ENOUGH TO MAKE LULU'S COMPUTER FEMALE.
--ONLINE--
HELLO, HANDSOME CHARLIE. WE'RE NOW TRAVELING NORTH BY NORTHWEST AT 280 MILES PER HOUR. WE ARE 467 MILES FROM OUR DESTINATION OF DENVER WHERE THE TEMPERATURE IS 47 DEGREES FAHRENHEIT.
WICKED COOL!
REDUCE SPEED TWENTY PERCENT TO ACCOMMODATE A FORTY DEGREE TURN.
WE'RE TURNING, BUT I CAN BARELY FEEL IT.

THERE'S A TILT MECHANISM TO KEEP US FROM JUMPING THE TRACK IN TIGHTER TURNS.
BUT, WE STILL CAN'T OPERATE AT TOP SPEED BECAUSE TRACK IMPROVEMENTS HAVEN'T KEPT UP WITH TRAIN TECH-NOLOGY.
YOU HELPED DESIGN ALL THIS?
HAH! ME?! NO. I CO-OWN CREDO INC., BUT I'M JUST A VERY RICH GLORIFIED CLERK.
MY BROTHER, BLAIRE IS THE BRAINS. HE'S THE GENIUS

THAT'S FOR SURE! HE THOUGHT OF EVERYTHING, INCLUDING MANUAL CONTROLS IN CASE ALL THIS TECHNOLOGY FAILS.
BLAIRE WORKED DAY AND NIGHT ON THIS TRAIN. HE'S A BRILLIANT INVENTOR AND ENGINEER...
LIKE ROY?
YES.
LIKE ROY.

ANYWAY! LET'S GET BACK TO THE OTHERS, SHALL WE?
YES! LET'S! I MEAN, CHOO-CHOO CHARLIE NEEDS TO CONCENTRATE ON HIS DRIVING.

THAT'S IT FOR THE TOUR! ANY QUESTIONS, LADIES?
I HAVE ONE!
IT FIGURES.
IF THIS TRAIN IS SO EFFICIENT AND FAST, WHY IS IT ONE OF A KIND? I MEAN WHY AREN'T OTHER TRAIN BUILDERS USING THIS TECH-NOLOGY?!
DEVELOPING PUBLIC TRANS-PORTATION IS VERY EXPENSIVE.
MY BROTHER ALMOST LANDED A BIG GOVERNMENT CONTRACT, BUT THEY TURNED US DOWN.

WHERE IS YOUR BROTHER? WHY ISN'T HE WORKING ON THIS TANK PROJECT?
YOU ASK A LOT OF QUESTIONS, DON'T YOU?
WELL, I AM A GIRL DETECTIVE.
YES, WELL, NOT GETTING THE CONTRACT HURT. HE'S TAKING TIME OFF TO RECOVER.
BUT I SMELL FOOD. LET'S SEE WHAT'S FOR LUNCH!

THEY MAY HAVE FAILED TO GET ENOUGH MONEY TO MASS PRODUCE THEIR AWESOME TRAIN, BUT CREDO INC. MANAGED TO SERVE UP THE TASTIEST ***FOOD*** I'D EVER HAD.

I THOUGHT WE SHOULD WAKE ROY AND HARRY FOR THIS FEAST, BUT RALPH THOUGHT IT BEST TO LET THEM SLEEP.

WHILE THE REST OF US WERE HAVING A GREAT TIME, DEIRDRE'S BOREDOM BECAME A FORCE TO BE RECKONED WITH.

DON'T LOOK NOW, BUT THERE'S A DORSAL FIN CIRCLING YOU WITH ITS ***EYES***.

HUH?!

POOR NED.
IT'S ALWAYS THE SWEET ONES WHO ATTRACT THE LAME HUNGRY PREDATORS.
POOR NED.
IT'S ALWAYS THE SWEET ONES WHO WIND UP SITTING WITH THEIR INSIPID GIRLFRIEND'S INSIPID FRIENDS.
KA CHAN KA

OH!
OH!
LOOK OUT!
OW!

YOU ALL RIGHT?
YEAH. THANKS FOR TRYING TO LESSEN THE BLOW. BUT, I'M STARTING TO BE PROUD OF MY GROWING BUMP COLLECTION.
YOU SHOULD HAVE KEPT YOUR HELMET ON!
YOU CAN'T REALLY EXPECT HER TO RISK HELMET-HAIR JUST TO KEEP FROM GETTING A LITTLE CONCUSSION.
I CAN'T BELIEVE YOU'RE WHINING ABOUT YOUR SILLY HEAD, WHEN MY HAUTE COUTURE IS RUINED.
ACTUALLY, THAT WAS BESS. I HADN'T THOUGHT ABOUT MY HAIR AT ALL. I JUST TOOK IT OFF SO I COULD SEE BETTER.
AND I WAS GLAD I DID. HATE TO ADMIT IT, BUT IT WAS KIND OF FUN SEEING DEIRDRE ALL SPLATTERED LIKE THAT.

SORRY EVERYONE. THE TRAIN JUST PROBABLY SWITCHED TRACKS.
THERE ARE FULL BATHS IN THE SLEEPING CAR, MISS SHANNON, IF YOU'D LIKE TO CLEAN UP.
YEAH, PLEASE QUARANTINE ALL CRANKINESS.
SWITCHING TRACKS? THEN WHY SERVE LUNCH NOW?
YOU'RE RIGHT. I EXPECTED A MUCH SMOOTHER TRACK TRANSITION FROM LULU!
YEAH, SOMETHING DOESN'T FEEL RIGHT.

WELL, EVEN WITH HEAD INJURIES WE ALL KNOW BETTER THAN TO NOT TRUST THOSE *FEELINGS* OF YOURS.
LET'S CHECK THE SYSTEM, SHALL WE?
IT'S EASY ENOUGH TO HACK INTO THE TRAIN'S LOVELY COMPUTER AND SCAN OUR PROGRESS.
LULU CAN TELL US *HERSELF* IF ANYTHING'S WRONG.
ONLINE

THEORETICALLY, WITH A LITTLE *MORE* HACKING, I COULD SEND THE TRAIN ANYWHERE I WANT... ANY PREFERENCES?

DISNEY WORLD WOULD BE NICE. BUT I GUESS WE'LL HAVE TO CONTENT OURSELVES WITH THE PROVINCIAL CHARM OF...

BISMARCK?!
BISMARCK
MY GEOGRAPHY ISN'T GREAT, BUT IS BISMARCK ON THE WAY FROM RIVER HEIGHTS TO *DENVER*?
BISMARCK
NOT ON ANY MAP I'VE EVER SEEN!
OKAY, GORGEOUS! *TALK*!
WE ARE CURRENTLY TRAVELING AT 240 MILES PER HOUR. WINDS NORTH BY NORTHEAST. WE ARE 100 MILES FROM OUR DESTINATION.

credo
File View Window Help
Colorado
ACCORDING TO THE TRAIN'S COMPUTER WE'RE SUPPOSED TO BE IN COLORADO, 100 MILES FROM DENVER!
REMEMBER HOW I SAID THAT *THEORETICALLY* I COULD HACK INTO THE SYSTEM AND TAKE THIS TRAIN ANYWHERE I WANTED TO.
YEAH?!
LET ME GUESS...

SOMEONE ACTUALLY DID HACK INTO THE COMPUTER...
...AND IS HIJACKING THE TRAIN!
END CHAPTER ONE

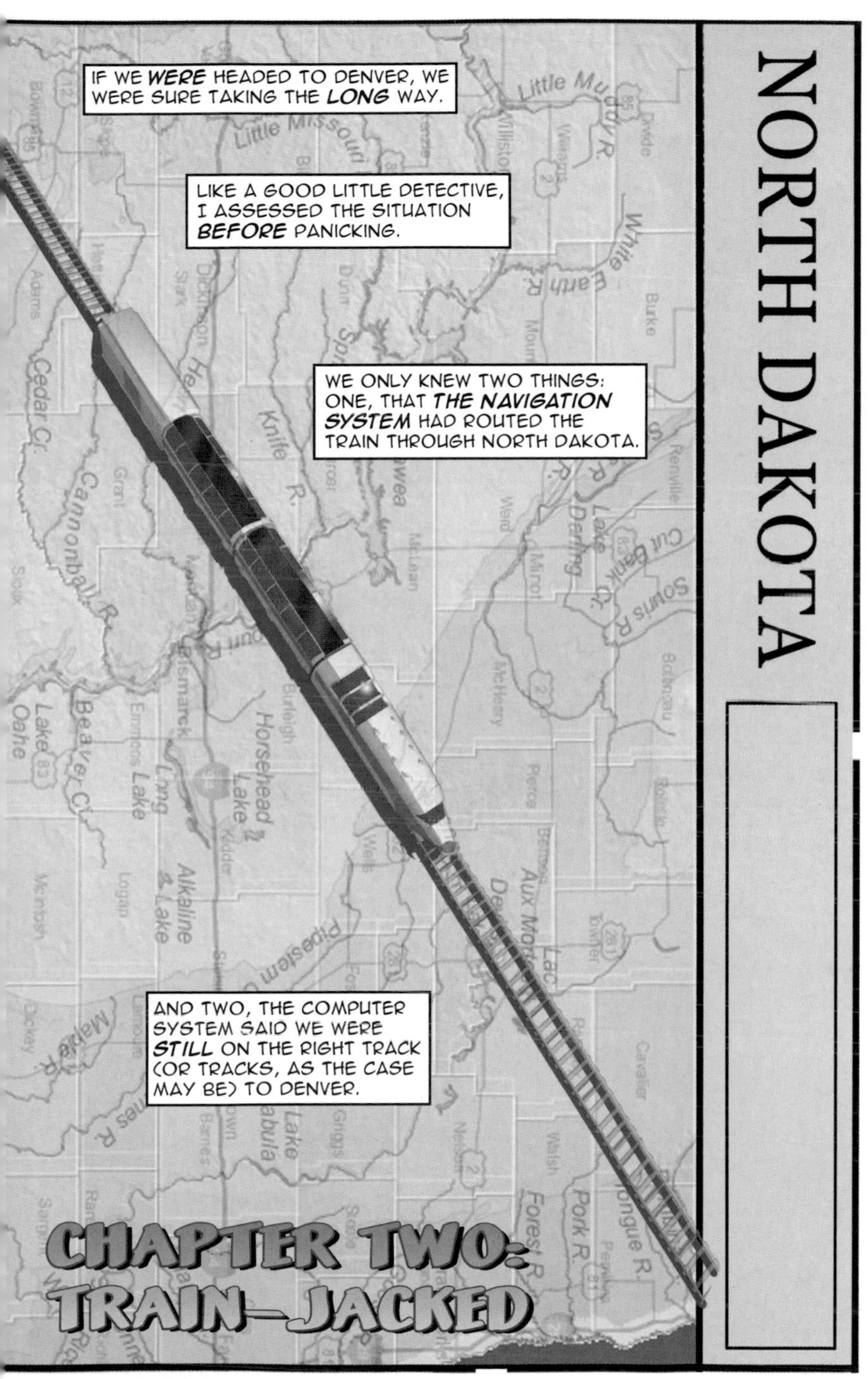
NORTH DAKOTA
IF WE WERE HEADED TO DENVER, WE WERE SURE TAKING THE LONG WAY.
LIKE A GOOD LITTLE DETECTIVE, I ASSESSED THE SITUATION BEFORE PANICKING.
WE ONLY KNEW TWO THINGS: ONE, THAT THE NAVIGATION SYSTEM HAD ROUTED THE TRAIN THROUGH NORTH DAKOTA.
AND TWO, THE COMPUTER SYSTEM SAID WE WERE STILL ON THE RIGHT TRACK (OR TRACKS, AS THE CASE MAY BE) TO DENVER.
CHAPTER TWO: TRAIN-JACKED

SO, BASED ON THE FACTS, THERE WERE TWO POSSIBILITIES...

...THAT WE WERE ON A RUNAWAY TRAIN, OR...
...WE WERE BEING HIJACKED!
WITH MY FACTS STRAIGHT, I DECIDED IT WAS COMPLETELY APPROPRIATE NOW TO PANIC.

I CAN'T GET THE TRAIN'S COMPUTER TO TELL ME ANYTHING BUT LIES. EITHER SHE'S BROKEN OR SOMEONE HAS DELIBERATELY MESSED WITH HER GPS RECEIVER.*
LULU SAYS DENVER! THAT'S HER STORY AND SHE'S STICKIN' TO IT! I WONDER IF SHE ACTUALLY BELIEVES WHAT SHE'S SAYING.
*THAT'S SHORT FOR GLOBAL POSITIONING SYSTEM, WHICH USES SATELLITE INFORMATION TO TELL YOU EXACTLY WHERE ON EARTH YOU ARE!
I THINK YOU AND LULU ARE GETTING TOO CLOSE, GEORGE.
LULU?
THAT'S CHARLIE, THE ENGINEER'S PET NAME FOR THE LOCOMOTIVE. NOW IT'S WHAT GEORGE CALLS THE COMPUTER LADY, TOO.
SHOULDN'T WE TALK TO THE REAL-LIFE ENGINEER?

OF COURSE. CHARLIE MUST HAVE NOTICED OUR SUDDEN DETOUR. MAYBE HE WAS EVEN THE ONE TAKING US FOR A RIDE. WHO KNEW THE TRAIN BETTER?
IF HE WAS GUILTY, I WASN'T SURE HOW SMART IT WAS FOR ME TO MARCH IN THERE AND QUESTION HIM.
RALPH CREDO WAS STILL IN BACK HELPING DEEDEE WITH HER DESIGNER TRAGEDY.
SHOULD I WAIT, OR TELL OUR HOST'S ASSISTANT, JOE BLANDER WHAT I KNEW?
HE DIDN'T SEEM TO HAVE NOTICED WE WERE GOING THE WRONG WAY NOW, AND HE DIDN'T REALLY WANT US THERE, SO HE PROBABLY WOULDN'T BE INCLINED TO BELIEVE ME ABOUT ANYTHING.
SO I THOUGHT MAYBE I WAS BETTER OFF DOING A LITTLE MORE THINKING.

I UNDERSTOOD WHY SOMEONE WOULD WANT TO STEAL THIS COOL TRAIN, ESPECIALLY WITH THE TOP SECRET ENGINE ON BOARD, BUT, REALLY, WHERE DID THEY THINK THEY COULD HIDE IT?
AND WHAT KIND OF NUT WOULD BE STUPID ENOUGH TO STEAL A TRAIN WHEN IT WAS FULL OF PEOPLE?
USUALLY A HIGHJACKER WANTS TO TRADE THE PLANE, BOAT OR TRAIN FOR SOMETHING. BUT, WE'D RECEIVED NO DEMANDS...
OR HAD WE?

MR. BLANDER?
YES... OH, IT'S YOU, WHAT IS IT? I'M VERY BUSY.
MAY I TALK TO YOU... PRIVATELY?
ANYTHING YOU HAVE TO SAY CAN BE SAID IN FRONT OF MR. SHANNON, YOUNG LADY.
YOUNG LADY?! I KNEW HE WASN'T DELIGHTED TO BE HOSTING THIS EXCURSION FOR RIVER HEIGHTS' YOUNG PEOPLE, BUT THERE WAS NO REASON TO BE CONDESCENDING.

FINE! THIS TRAIN IS BEING...
...WELL LET'S JUST SAY WE'RE OFF COURSE.
WHAT?!
LET'S RELAX, SHALL WE?
THAT'S A LITTLE HARD WHEN WE'RE HEADING NORTH WHEN WE'RE SUPPOSED TO BE GOING WEST.
I'M SURE IT'S JUST A MISTAKE. I'LL GO SEE CHARLIE.
COULD YOU ALSO ASK HIM WHY WE'RE NOT SLOWING DOWN WHEN WE PASS THROUGH TOWNSHIPS?
WE BLEW THROUGH THE LAST TOWN AT WAY OVER THE LIMIT.

GOOD HEAVENS!
YOU DON'T SUPPOSE THE TRAIN IS BEING HIJACKED?! I'M GOING TO FIND MY DAUGHTER AND TELL MR. CREDO.
UH, MR. SHANNON, ARE YOU SURE YOU WANT TO ALARM DEIRDRE, JUST YET?!
IF I NEED YOUR ADVICE, I'LL--
I HAVE AWAKENED! YOU MAY BE HAPPY AGAIN!
AND WHO THE HECK ARE YOU?
DID I MISS LUNCH?

I WOULD HAVE SLEPT LONGER, TRUTH BE TOLD! BUT, SOME SOBBING WENCH WOKE ME.
THAT'S MY DAUGHTER.
WELL, SHE'S LOCKED HERSELF IN THE BATHROOM AND IS CRYING LIKE YOU FLUSHED HER PET TURTLE.
I OFFERED HELP AND SHE CURSED ME LIKE A SAILOR. YOU SHOULD TALK TO HER ABOUT THAT MOUTH OF HERS.
SEE? AT LEAST *I* DIDN'T SAY IT.

EXCUSE ME!
CREDO MUST HAVE HIS OWN SLEEPER COMPARTMENT. HARD TO BELIEVE HE AND HARRY COULD NAP THROUGH THAT RACKET.
WHO'S NAPPING? WHO THE HECK ARE YOU?! DID I MISS LUNCH?
!
YOU GENTLEMEN HAVE MISSED QUITE A *BIT*, I'M AFRAID.

I'D JUST GIVEN HARRY AND ROY THE HEADS UP ABOUT OUR MYSTERIOUS DETOUR WHEN JOE DISCOVERED HE COULDN'T OPEN THE DOOR TO THE OBSERVATION DECK.
ACK! IT'S JAMMED!
NON-SENSE. COME ON, SON. YOU LOOK LIKE A STRONG YOUNG FELLOW.
HE'S VERY STRONG, FOR A LIT MAJOR!
UNNNGH!
INGNNGH!

FORTUNATELY, WE COULD SEE ALL THE WAY THROUGH TO THE ENGINE CAR.
THERE'S CHARLIE SITTING IN HIS CHAIR.
BUT, SOMETHING'S STRANGE ABOUT HIM.
WHAT? WHAT'S STRANGE?
WELL, HE'S NOT MOVING.
GEE, I GUESS EVEN THE MOST RELIABLE WORKER TAKES A NAP ON THE JOB, OCCASIONALLY, BUT...
I'M NOT BUYING THAT, BESS, AND NEITHER ARE YOU.

I GUESS IT WAS THE MOST INTERESTING THING GOING ON, BUT THAT WINDOW STARTED GETTING *CROWDED*.
IF WE ARE BEING HIJACKED BY A COMPUTER HACKER, THE CROOK WOULD HAVE TO MAKE *SURE* CHARLIE COULDN'T OVERRIDE THE SYSTEM MANUALLY!
COULD THEY *DISABLE* THE MANUAL OVERRIDE ON THE COMPUTER?
I DON'T KNOW.
UMM... ACTUALLY, I WAS ASKING *GEORGE*.

I GUESS THEY COULD. I DON'T SEE WHY NOT, IF THEY KNOW THE SYSTEM.
BUT, THE ONLY SURE WAY TO **KNOW** IF THEY ***DID***, IS TO TRY THE MANUAL CONTROLS.
WE HAVE TO GET THROUGH THAT DOOR, HARRY.
WE COULD REALLY USE YOUR EXPERT ***LOCKPICKING*** SKILLS ABOUT NOW.
YOU MEAN, ***WITHOUT*** LUNCH?

FIVE MINUTES LATER, HARRY HAD THE DOOR OPEN.
IT WAS LOCKED FROM THE OTHER SIDE.
CLICK
A SECOND LATER, JOE BLANDER WAS RUSHING INTO THE ENGINE ROOM.
I'LL GO SEE IF CHARLIE'S OKAY.
I SHOULD GO ALONE!
I'LL HAVE TO INSIST YOU WAIT HERE!

WAIT HERE?
IS HE KIDDING OR WHAT?
YOU KNOW THAT'S NOT GOING TO HAPPEN.
AFTER YOU, LASSIE.
THANK YOU, SIR!

WAY TO LISTEN, PEOPLE.
IS HE OKAY?
I WAS PERFECTLY FINE AND THEN SUDDENLY, WHAM.
SOMEONE BOPPED YOU ON THE BEAN?!
NO! I JUST PASSED OUT!
I STILL FEEL ALL ACHY, LIKE I'VE BEEN DRUGGED, BUT HOW? WHY?

WHO BROUGHT YOU THAT LUNCH?
I DID. IT'S ONE OF MY... DUTIES WHEN WE'RE TRAVELLING.
SNIFF
AND I COMPLETELY TRUST THE COOK AND WAITER. THEY'VE BEEN WITH US FOR YEARS.

I'D HAVE TO DEAL WITH THE DRUGGED LUNCH LATER. RIGHT THEN, I TOLD CHARLIE TO TRY TO OVERRIDE THE SYSTEM USING THE MANUAL CONTROLS.

BUT IT WAS NO GOOD. THE TRAIN JUST KEPT BARRELING ON TOWARD WHO KNOWS WHERE.

RADIO COMMUNICATION WITH UNION PACIFIC DISPATCH WASN'T HAPPENING, EITHER.
FSSSHHHH

WE KEPT CHECKING OUR CELLS FOR A SIGNAL.

NO SIGNAL

BUT, FOR NOW, WE WEREN'T GETTING ANYONE ON THE ***PHONE***.

TRAINS DON'T SWITCH TRACKS BY THEMSELVES. AND ACCORDING TO MY MAP, GETTING HERE WOULD HAVE REQUIRED SWITCHING TRACKS TWICE.
I DON'T SUPPOSE ONE OF YOU COMPANY MEN KNOWS HOW A SMART GAL WITH A LAPTOP MIGHT TAP INTO THE SYSTEM AND GET US HEADED BACK IN THE RIGHT DIRECTION.
A SECRET ACCESS CODE, OR SOME-THING?
NO. UNTIL NOW, THERE WAS NEVER ANY NEED FOR A SECURITY CODE.
AND DON'T BOTHER ASKING RALPH. HE HIRED ME SO HE'D NEVER HAVE TO FIGURE OUT HOW TO TURN ON A COMPUTER.
WE'LL HAVE TO GET INTO THE SYSTEM SOMEHOW.
IF YOU TWO HAVE NO IDEAS, GEORGE WILL HAVE TO WORK HER OWN SPECIAL MAGIC.

CHARLIE ASSURED US HE WAS *FINE* AND HE'D KEEP TRYING TO CONTACT UNION PACIFIC DISPATCH AND OVERRIDE THE SYSTEM, MANUALLY.

I'D BETTER GO TELL MR. CREDO.
OUR BEST HOPE FOR REGAINING CONTROL OF THE TRAIN NOW WAS GEORGE. WHEN SHE WAS *FOCUSED*, GEORGE COULD HACK ANY COMPUTER SYSTEM.

WELL, I MANAGED TO GET A *FEW SECONDS* OF INTERNET ACCESS AS WE SPED THROUGH THAT LAST TOWN, BUT *LOST* IT BEFORE I COULD GET A SINGLE E-MAIL OFF. I'LL KEEP TRYING.
YOU HAVE CONNECTION.
INTERNET

IS IT TRUE?! ARE WE REALLY BEING HIJACKED?!
BUT... SO MUCH FOR FOCUS.
NED! PLEASE! TELL ME THE TRUTH!
OKAY. WE'RE TAKEN OFF COURSE, BUT WE DON'T KNOW HOW OR WHY YET. I'M SURE NANCY WILL FIGURE IT OUT.
NANCY, NANCY, NANCY!
WHAT IF IT'S SOME WHACKO WHO DOESN'T WANT ANYTHING EXCEPT TO HURT INNOCENT PEOPLE?
LIKE ME!

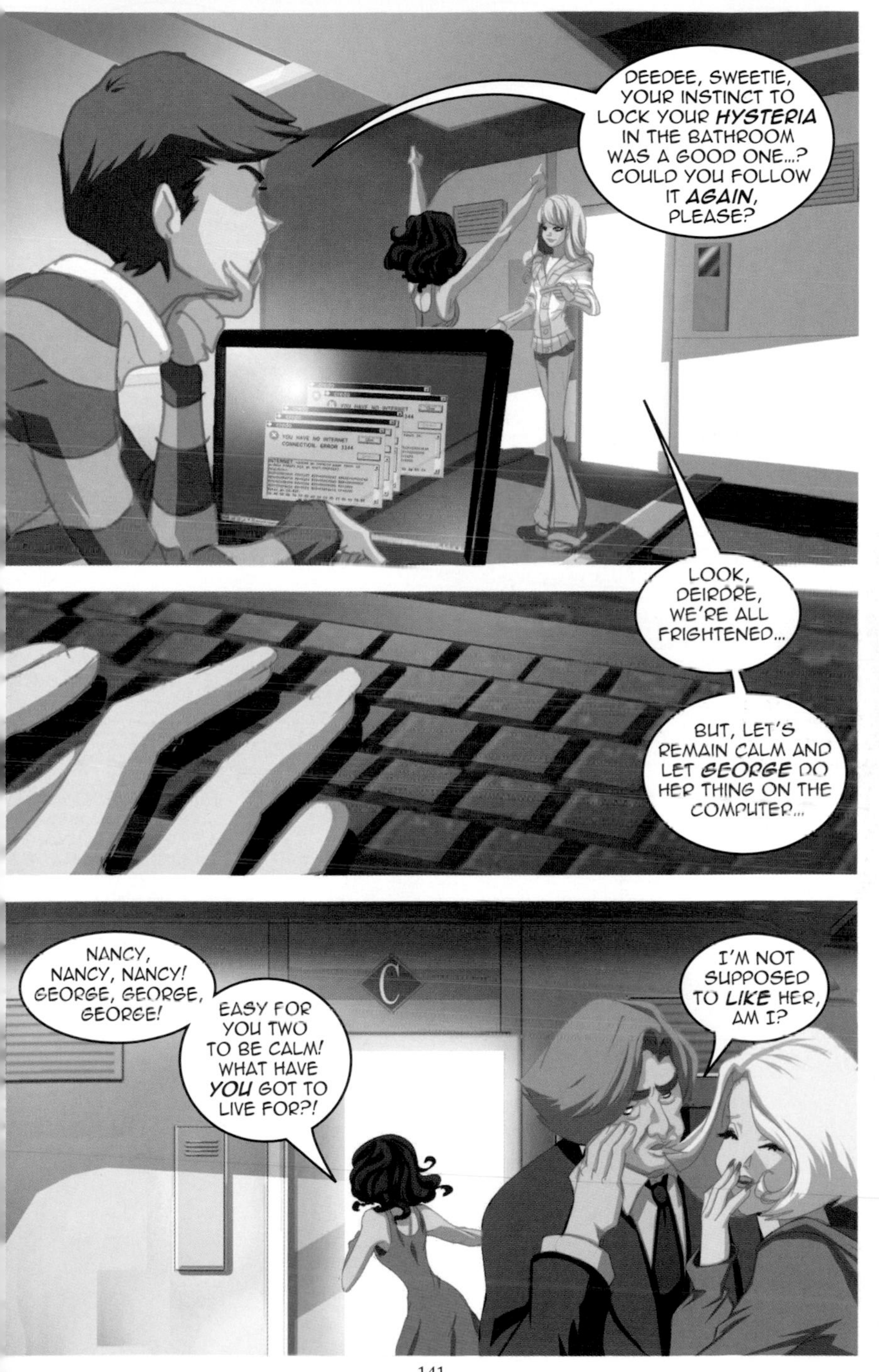
DEEDEE, SWEETIE, YOUR INSTINCT TO LOCK YOUR HYSTERIA IN THE BATHROOM WAS A GOOD ONE...? COULD YOU FOLLOW IT AGAIN, PLEASE?
YOU HAVE NO INTERNET CONNECTION. ERROR 3344
LOOK, DEIRDRE, WE'RE ALL FRIGHTENED...
BUT, LET'S REMAIN CALM AND LET GEORGE DO HER THING ON THE COMPUTER...
NANCY, NANCY, NANCY! GEORGE, GEORGE, GEORGE!
EASY FOR YOU TWO TO BE CALM! WHAT HAVE YOU GOT TO LIVE FOR?!
I'M NOT SUPPOSED TO LIKE HER, AM I?

OKAY! WHAT HAVE YOU GOT?
WELL, THERE'S CREEPY NEWS, GOOD NEWS AND BAD NEWS.
CREEPY NEWS IS THAT THE ONLY WAY TO HAVE CONTINUOUS ACCESS TO LULU'S TRACK SWITCHING PROGRAM IS THROUGH THE TRAIN'S LOCAL NETWORK, MEANING THE HIJACKER HAS TO BE EITHER MOVING ALONG WITH US AT CLOSE RANGE OR ON THE TRAIN.
GOOD NEWS IS I THINK I KNOW HOW TO CONTROL LULU'S SWITCHER.
AND THE BAD?
WELL, BASED ON THE VISUAL CUES TELLING WHERE WE ARE AND ON HOW FAST WE'RE GOING, I CAN KIND OF ASSESS WHERE WE'RE HEADED...
WAIT, ISN'T THAT GOOD NEWS?
UH... MAYBE, MAYBE NOT.
DURING A FLEETING MOMENT OF INTERNET SERVICE, I DOWNLOADED SOME SATELLITE PHOTOS OF THIS AREA...

SOON, WE'LL HIT A FORK.
THERE OUR MYSTERY HIJACKER COULD TAKE US ONE OF TWO WAYS...
"ONE WAY TAKES US TO THIS CUTE LITTLE QUARRY TOWN. THAT WOULD BE GOOD.

"THE OTHER WAY TAKES US TO A HUGE, ABANDONED QUARRY."
"THERE'S ANOTHER FORK NEAR THE QUARRY."
"ONE WAY TAKES US SAFELY TO THE BOTTOM OF THE QUARRY ON PERFECTLY GOOD TRACKS. THIS IS ALSO GOOD."

AND THE OTHER WAY?
ailRoads Information cen
th dakota
YOU JUST HAD TO ASK...
"THOSE TRACKS SEEM TO COLLAPSE..."
CAUTION! TRACKS END!

I STOPPED GEORGE.

SHE DIDN'T NEED TO FINISH THE SENTENCE. IT WOULDN'T BE WISE TO MAKE A GENERAL ANNOUNCEMENT THAT ONE OF OUR TWO POSSIBLE DESTINATIONS WAS...

...THE EDGE OF A HUGE CLIFF!!

END CHAPTER TWO

AS MUCH AS IT PAINED ME, THAT CLIFF MADE ME THINK DEEDEE MIGHT BE RIGHT...
...THIS MIGHT BE THE WORK OF A CRAZY PERSON WHO GOT HIS KICKS HURTING INNOCENT PEOPLE.
SOOOBBB
VRRRRRR
BUT, I DIDN'T FEEL I HAD THE LUXURY OF LOCKING MYSELF IN THE BATHROOM.
SOOOBBB

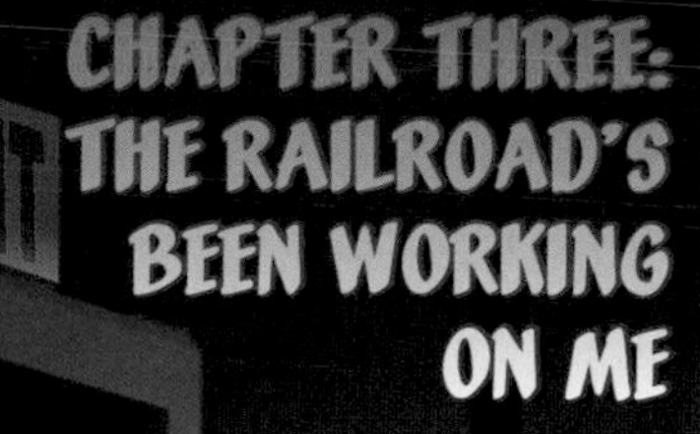
CHAPTER THREE:
THE RAILROAD'S BEEN WORKING ON ME

SOME OF US HAD TO FIGURE OUT HOW TO STOP THIS TRAIN.
NED SEEMED TO HAVE NERVES OF STEEL. HE JUST SAT READING.
THE REST OF US PACED WHAT LITTLE FLOOR THERE WAS, WAITING FOR SOME HOPE FROM GEORGE WHO DILIGENTLY PROBED LULU FOR ACCESS TO THE TRAIN'S CONTROLS.
OKAY, THAT'S IT!

WHAT?!
JUST BACK OFF, AND I'LL TELL YOU WHERE WE'RE AT.
SORRY. WE'RE COOL.
SIGH
LULU IS BEING STUBBORN. THERE'S NO WAY FOR ME TO GAIN CONTROL OF THE BRAKES OR THE TRACK SWITCHES USING THE COMPUTER.
YOU CAN'T?!

WHAT DO YOU SUGGEST?
WARNING 0356 DISABLING PROGRAM IN 28 SECONDS.
WARNING
TAP
I'M SHUTTING LULU DOWN, SENDING A VIRUS TO THE PROGRAM SO NO ONE ELSE CAN USE IT! THIS SHOULD GIVE CHARLIE BACK MANUAL CONTROL.
I HOPE, UNION PACIFIC HAS FIGURED OUT WE'RE A RENEGADE TRAIN AND WILL COME SAVE US. WE COULD SEND UP A FLARE, BUT IT'D ONLY BE SEEN BY THE BUFFALO.
AND HAVEN'T WE HURT THEM ENOUGH?
CHARLIE SHOULD HAVE MANUAL CONTROL BY NOW. LET'S SEE HOW HE'S DOING.
AND HOW CLOSE WE ARE TO THAT FORK IN OUR FATE.

YOU GO ON AHEAD.
JOE'S BEEN GONE A LONG TIME FINDING CREDO. I'M GOING TO FIND OUT WHAT'S KEEPING HIM.
I'D BETTER CHECK OUT THE EMERGENCY EXITS, TOO. IF IT BECOMES NECESSARY, I CAN IMAGINE ALMOST EVERYONE ABOARD JUMPING FROM THE SPEEDING TRAIN...
JUMPING?
WE'D BREAK ALL THE BONES IN OUR BODIES JUMPING AT THIS SPEED.
SOUND'S LESS THAN FUN. BUT, CHARLIE SHOULD BE ABLE TO SLOW DOWN NOW THAT THE COMPUTER'S DISABLED.
I'LL TELL MR. CREDO.

ONE OF THE EMERGENCY EXITS WAS THROUGH THE BATHROOM WHERE DEIRDRE WAS HOLED UP. TO GET HER OUT, MR. SHANNON HAD RESORTED TO BEGGING.
C'MON, SWEETHEART! IF YOU COME OUT *NOW*, DADDY WILL BUY YOU SOMETHING NICE AND EXPENSIVE.
RESTROOM
NO!
SEEING ME, HE TRIED TO PUT ON A LESS PATHETIC FRONT.
UH, DEIRDRE SHANNON, YOU COME OUT OF THERE RIGHT THIS MINUTE, YOUNG LADY!
WHAT?! WAAAAH!

I, UH, WAS JUST LOOKING FOR MR. CREDO AND MR. BLANDER.
JOE JUST WENT INTO THE SECOND DOOR ON THE RIGHT.

MR. CREDO? ARE YOU ALL RIGHT?
IN RALPH CREDO'S SLEEPING COMPARTMENT, THE SCENE WAS STRANGELY FAMILIAR.

FINE, NANCY. I JUST HAD TROUBLE WAKING UP. MY HEAD FEELS LIKE LEAD. APPARENTLY, I SLEPT THROUGH A LOT!
JOE'S TOLD ME OF OUR DIRE PREDICA-MENT.

YES. GEORGE DISABLED THE COMPUTER'S CONTROL, SO CHARLIE SHOULD BE ABLE TO USE THE MANUAL CONTROLS.
AT THIS POINT IT'S PROBABLY BEST TO SIMPLY SLOW DOWN ENOUGH TO LET EVERYONE OFF, SINCE WE CAN'T TELL IF ANOTHER TRAIN IS COMING.
CREDO
WHOA!
WHAT?!
CREDO
THAT WAS THE SECOND TIME I'D FOUND A SPENT PACK OF SMELLING SALTS. MY TIMING WAS BAD, THOUGH, SINCE CHARLIE PICKED THAT MOMENT TO SLOW THE TRAIN DOWN.
BUMP
CREDO
OW!

GEE, GREAT NEWS. I'LL MAKE SURE EVERYONE IS READY TO DISEMBARK AND GET SOME ICE FOR YOUR HEAD.
I'M OKAY, MR. BLANDER, REALLY?
HE SEEMS MORE NERVOUS NOW THAN **BEFORE** WE KNEW WE'D BE GETTING OFF THE TRAIN.
JOE'S INSCRUTABLE!
AHHHHHH!
A BLOOD CURDLING SCREAM FROM DOWN THE HALL MADE ME WONDER IF **ANYONE** WAS TAKING THE GOOD NEWS WELL.

IT'S A NIGHT-MARE!
WHAT HAPPENED MR. SHANNON? IS DEIRDRE ALL RIGHT?
WELL, WHEN THE TRAIN SLOWED, DEIRDRE DROPPED HER HAIRDRYER...
I DROPPED THE HAIRDRYER IN THE TOILET!
NOW HOW WILL I DRY MY DRESS?!
WELL... WOULD IT MAKE YOU FEEL BETTER TO KNOW WE'RE PROBABLY GOING TO LIVE THROUGH THIS HIJACKING?

OW!
WE'RE SPEEDING UP AGAIN!
IT WAS ALL A **TRICK** JUST TO GET ME OUT OF THE BATH-ROOM! WE'RE ALL GOING TO DIE AND I HAVE NOTHING TO WEAR!
I'M **NEVER** COMING OUT!

WHAT'S GOING ON?
I DON'T KNOW!
JOE BLANDER RUSHED THROUGH TO THE LOCOMOTIVE A COUPLE OF MINUTES AGO AND A MINUTE LATER WE WERE SPEEDING UP AGAIN!
YOU GIRLS HAD BETTER SEE THIS. HARRY, YOU COME, TOO. AND BRING YOUR *TOOLS*! I CAN'T OPEN THE OTHER DOOR TO THE LOCOMOTIVE.

GASP!
WE HAVE TO GET THIS DOOR OPEN!
I CAN'T GET THROUGH THIS DOOR.
WHAT?!

IT WAS BARRICADED! EVEN OUR EXPERT SAFECRACKER WAS POWERLESS.
I THOUGHT YOU SAID JOE WENT IN HERE...
I DON'T SEE HIM. HE VANISHED!
DID JOE GET SCARED AND JUMP OR DID THE HIJACKER THROW HIM FROM THE TRAIN?
ANOTHER MYSTERY, AND ANOTHER WORRY...
...THE SIGNAL AHEAD. I COULDN'T BE SURE WHAT IT MEANT, BUT I HAD A BAD FEELING WE WERE CLOSE TO THAT FORK IN THE TRACKS.
AND I HAD A BAD FEELING THAT WE WERE NOT GOING TO TAKE THE TRACKS LEADING TO THE NICE LITTLE TOWN.
ROY, IS THERE ANY WAY SOMEONE COULD DRIVE THE TRAIN AND SWITCH TRACKS WITHOUT USING A COMPUTER OR MANUAL CONTROLS?

WELL, I'M NOT REALLY A TRAIN MAN, BUT I SUPPOSE IT'S CONCEIVABLE THEY COULD USE A **REMOTE CONTROL** DEVICE, LIKE FOR A TOY TRAIN.
I SUDDENLY REALIZED THAT WE HAD TO DO AT LEAST ONE OF **TWO** IMPORTANT TASKS...
WE HAVE TO **STOP** WHOEVER'S DOING THIS BEFORE THEY DRIVE THIS THING OFF A CLIFF **OR** GET EVERYONE, INCLUDING GEORGE AND CHARLIE, OFF THE TRAIN BEFORE THAT HAPPENS!
WITH ANY LUCK, WE'LL DO **BOTH**.

ALL THE COMPARTMENTS WERE EMPTY.
EXCEPT ONE.

NOW, YOU WAIT JUST A MINUTE, YOU RUFFIAN!
SORRY, YOU LAWYER, BUT THIS IS THE LAST PLACE THE HIJACKER COULD BE HIDING AND I'M GOIN' IN.
RESTRO
DADDY! MAKE THEM STOP! I'M ALONE, I SWEAR.
ANY EVIL-DOER WOULD MAKE HER SAY THAT.
NOOOO!
CRASH

HOW DARE YOU?!
WHAT IS THIS? WERE YOU TRYING TO COMMIT SUICIDE OVER A DRESS?
DEIRDRE WAS ALONE. BUT, ASIDE FROM ROY'S ENJOYMENT, THERE WAS ANOTHER IMPORTANT REASON FOR BUSTING IN ON HER. THE EMERGENCY EXIT.
DEIRDRE, COME!
BUT, DADDY! MY DRESS!
SORRY, DEIRDRE! BUT, WE'VE GOT TO GET TO THE LOCO-MOTIVE.
WE?

NANCY, LET ME GO.
WE SHOULD BOTH GO, NED...JUST IN CASE.
NO, NED! DON'T GO!
NANCY IS REALLY GOOD AT THIS SORT OF THING. WHY RISK BOTH YOUR LIVES?
THANKS FOR YOUR CONCERN. BUT I PROMISE, WE'LL BOTH BE BACK.
AND I'LL STAY HERE TO MAKE SURE YOU BEHAVE.

THE WIND VELOCITY ALONE WAS GOING TO MAKE OUT-DOOR TRAIN TRAVEL TOUGH.
BUT, THIS WAS THE ONLY WAY TO GET TO GEORGE AND CHARLIE IN THE LOCOMOTIVE AND STOP THE TRAIN...
...AND FAST.
OUR LAST FORK WAS COMING UP!
123
E-32
SP-TRANSPORT
U.S.A
REDO LINE

WELL, THE WHO PART OF THE MYSTERY WAS SOLVED.
IT WAS JOE!
JOE WAS STILL ABOARD AND OBVIOUSLY IN POSSESSION OF A REMOTE CONTROL... MY GUESS, FOR THE TRAIN.
HE MUST HAVE JAMMED THE LOCOMOTIVE DOOR FROM THE INSIDE THEN CLIMBED OUT THROUGH THE HATCH TO THE ROOF.
THERE WASN'T TIME TO FIND OUT WHY JOE SEEMED TO WANT US ALL CRUSHED AT THE BOTTOM OF A QUARRY. WE JUST HAD TO GET THAT CONTROL.
JOE BLANDER!
123
SP-TRANSPORT
U.S.A
LINE

YOU TURN UP EVERYWHERE, DON'T YOU?
STAY WHERE YOU ARE. I MUST UNCOUPLE THE TRAIN SO ONLY THE TANK GOES OVER THE CLIFF.
EVERYONE WILL BE SAFE AS LONG AS I SWITCH TRACKS AND UNCOUPLE THE LAST CAR AT THE PRECISE MOMENT.
WHY? WHY DESTROY THE TANK?!
I'VE GOT MY REASONS.

BUT, WHAT IF IT DOESN'T WORK? IF THE CARS GO IN DIFFERENT DIRECTIONS WITHOUT UNCOUPLING, THE WHOLE TRAIN WILL DERAIL AND ROLL INTO THE QUARRY.
IT WILL BE FINE, I TELL YOU! NOW, I HAVE A JOB TO DO. SO, YOU MEDDLING KIDS SHOULD BEAT IT!
GIVE ME THAT!
SWING
BONK
CRASHH

WE STILL HAVE TO GET TO THE LOCOMOTIVE AND USE THE MANUAL CONTROLS TO STOP THE TRAIN.
NANCY, WAIT FOR *ME*!

JOE KNEW HE WAS BEATEN. NOW HIS ONLY HOPE WAS THE SAME AS OURS, TO SAVE THE WHOLE TRAIN, TANK AND ALL.
NED, WE HAVE TO CROSS THE GLASS ONE AT A TIME, SO IT DOESN'T...

CRACK?!
CRAAAACKKKK
NEVER MIND!

YOU NEVER KNOW HOW FAST YOU CAN MOVE, UNTIL YOU HAVE TO!
EEEEEP!
YOU CAN'T CROSS THE GLASS! IT'S TOO DANGEROUS!
GO BACK THROUGH THE BATHROOM. I'LL HANDLE THIS MYSELF.
I WAS SO WORRIED ABOUT GEORGE, I IMMEDIATELY USED WHAT WAS LEFT OF THOSE SMELLING SALTS TO REVIVE HER.
UHNN! SHOULDN'T YOU BE WAKING CHARLIE?
IT'S ALL RIGHT! I HAVE ANOTHER LEFT OVER SMELLING SALT.
BUT CHARLIE DIDN'T WAKE UP, MAYBE BECAUSE HE WAS BIGGER AND NEEDED MORE SMELLING SALTS. IT WAS ONLY THEN I REALIZED IT WOULD HAVE BEEN A GOOD IDEA TO WAKE THE ENGINEER FIRST!
UH - OH.

GRRRNNNGG
BUT, THERE WASN'T TIME FOR REGRETS!
SCREEEEEE
OW!
I WASN'T SURE, BUT, I THOUGHT I ACTUALLY HEARD THE TRAIN SIGH WITH RELIEF...
SCREEEEEE
...MAYBE IT WAS ME.

MR. BLANDER CLAIMS HE NEVER WANTED TO HARM ANY-ONE. HE SAYS HE WAS JUST *PAID* TO SEND THE TANK CAR OFF THE CLIFF TO STOP YOUR *TANK PROJECT*, WHATEVER *THAT* IS.
PAID? BY WHOM?
ABOUT THAT, HE'S NOT TALKING.
I CAN *MAKE* HIM TALK.
LET THE *LAW* HANDLE IT.
ALTHOUGH, *I* WOULD SURE HAVE LIKED SOME ANSWERS, TOO.

DADDY! I INSIST YOU SUE CREDO FOR ALL THE EMOTIONAL DAMAGE I HAVE SUFFERED!
UH-OH. EMOTIONAL DAMAGE IS A CONDITION SHE CAN CERTAINLY PROVE.
EMERGENCY
AND THIS DRESS! IT WILL NEVER BE THE SAME. I WANT IT REPLACED BY CREDO!
IF ROY CAN'T MAKE JOE TALK, CAN I PLEASE MAKE DEIRDRE STOP TALKING?!
NOPE! I DON'T THINK YOU CAN!
SO THE PASSENGERS AND THE TANK WERE ALL SAFE AND SOUND! THAT LEFT THE QUESTION OF JOE'S EMPLOYER, BUT THAT WAS SOMETHING I'D DEAL WITH NEXT TIME!

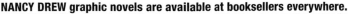

DISCARD